MW00647251
RIUS
Too Many Losing Heroines!

STAKE OUT
INFIDEL
INVE

STIGATION

"Eat up, Oniisama!"
KAJU-STYLE PANCAKES

IN THE BATH
FLUB-A-DUB-DUB

LOSERS

CONTENTS

Too Many Losing Heroines!

NOVEL

2

WRITTEN BY
Takibi Amamori

ILLUSTRATED BY
Imigimuru

Seven Seas Entertainment

MAKE HEROINE GA OSUGIRU! Vol. 2
by Takibi AMAMORI

Illustrations by Imigimuru

Original Japanese edition published by SHOGAKUKAN.
English translation rights in the United States of America, Canada, the United Kingdom, Ireland, Australia and New Zealand arranged with SHOGAKUKAN through Tuttle-Mori Agency, Inc.

Seven Seas press and purchase enquiries can be sent to Marketing Manager Lauren Hill at press@gomanga.com. Information regarding the distribution and purchase of digital editions is available from Digital Manager CK Russell at digital@gomanga.com.

Follow Seven Seas Entertainment online at sevenseasentertainment.com.

TRANSLATION: Matthew Jackson
ADAPTATION: Acro
COVER DESIGN: H. Qi
INTERIOR LAYOUT & DESIGN: Clay Gardner
COPY EDITOR: Jade Gardner
PROOFREADER: Catherine Pedigo
EDITOR: Callum May
PREPRESS TECHNICIAN: Melanie Ujimori, Jules Valera
MANAGING EDITOR: Alyssa Scavetta
EDITOR-IN-CHIEF: Julie Davis
PUBLISHER: Lianne Sentar
VICE PRESIDENT: Adam Arnold
PRESIDENT: Jason DeAngelis

ISBN: 979-8-89160-308-0
Printed in Canada
First Printing: November 2024
10 9 8 7 6 5 4 3 2 1

CHARACTERS

LOSERS AND FRIENDS

Nukumizu Kazuhiko
First-year. Proud loner.

Yanami Anna
First-year. Happy and hungry.

Komari Chika
First-year. Lit club. A bit far gone.

Yakishio Lemon
First-year. Fastest & loudest girl on the track team.

Nukumizu Kaju
Second-year, junior high. Little sister from heaven.

Tsukinoki Koto
Third-year. Vice president of the lit club.

Shikiya Yumeko
Second-year. Student council. Most fashionable zombie.

Tamaki Shintarou
Third-year. President of the lit club.

Ayano Mitsuki
First-year. Brainiac bookworm.

Asagumo Chihaya
First-year. Ayano's girlfriend.

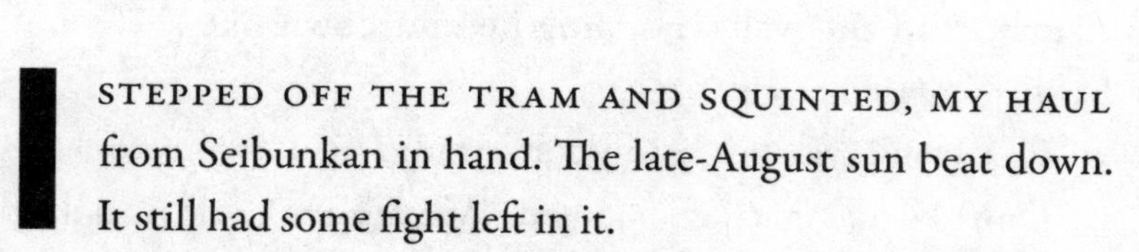

I STEPPED OFF THE TRAM AND SQUINTED, MY HAUL from Seibunkan in hand. The late-August sun beat down. It still had some fight left in it.

The weight of the book in my hand and the matte feel of the cover against my fingers brought a smile to my face as I crossed the street. How could it not? I'd waited for what felt like forever, and now it was finally here. The latest release of *Call Me Flat, Step in Crap*—an action novel set in a dystopian reality wherein one's chest size determines their status in society. The previous volume had ended on the *worst* cliffhanger, in which it was revealed that the protagonist's best friend and confidant, Kirari-chan, had not only grown to C-cup, but was now the enemy.

It was just before noon, and Nukumizu Kazuhiko of Tsuwabuki High School's class 1-C, member of the literature club—that is to say, *I*—was very excited to spend another boring day of summer vacation in blessed air conditioning.

Bidding farewell to the noisy cicadas behind me, I stepped through the front door.

"Welcome home, my dearest Oniisama!"

My little sister, Kaju, came running over in denim overalls and a cute ribbon poking out from her long black hair. "Cute" was a good word for her. Aside from her tendency to hyper fixate on every little thing I did, which was decidedly *un*cute.

"Where's the fire?" I asked.

"Oh, it's worse than fire!"

Kaju held out a calendar (which I could only assume she'd snatched off the wall), hopping up and down like she could hardly contain herself.

"Flammable, yes, but hardly concerning."

"Don't be like that!" she pouted. "We need to settle on a date for the interview, like, *now*! Actually, I like the sound of that. Now is the perfect time!"

I very much knew exactly what she was talking about.

"I've got a better idea," I said. "First, breathe. Second, chill out. Use your words."

"You're so right, Oniisama! So there I was, getting lunch ready, when a knock came—oh, we're having yesterday's curry, for the record."

Baby steps, I thought. We'd extract a full sentence out of her at some point.

"Curry's always better on day two, for sure." I nodded. "So we have company?"

"Yes! That! Gosh, and I'm not even presentable! I need you to entertain while I go get changed!"

"Say what now?"

"Living room!" Kaju blurted as she bolted up the stairs.

Who were we having over? Royalty? I bent down to straighten my shoes at the door, and that was when I noticed it. Another pair I didn't recognize. Distinctly feminine. Too big for Kaju, and far too trendy for our mom.

I turned my head and stared down the hallway. "No..."

With intrepid steps, I ventured forth.

Too Many Losing Heroines!

Yanami Anna Goes Fishing

"HELLO?"

Beyond the door, as it creaked open, lay unchanged scenery. Our combined living and dining rooms were as they were, a spacious eighteen tatami mats in size. Some rerun of a travel show played on the TV. All was as it should be.

If it weren't for the girl currently occupying a seat at the table.

"Hey, Nukumizu-kun! Good to see ya again!" The intruder opened her mouth wide and chomped down on a mountainous spoonful of curry.

"What in the world are you doing here?!"

Yanami Anna. Current status: cheeks puffed full of rice and roux, recently had her man stolen by a fresh-off-the-plane transfer student, a losing heroine if ever there was one.

She swallowed, failed to notice the rice on her cheek, and grinned at me. "This curry's good. It usually is after the second day, huh?"

"Right. So are you gonna tell me why you're in my house eating said curry?"

"Oh, mwuhmfm."

Please swallow.

Well, with that, the identity of the mystery guest was no longer a mystery. I took a seat across from her, sighing. A moment later, she finished chewing. Thank god.

"You really gotta tell me in advance *before* you show up," I said.

Yanami was unamused by such reasonable expectations. "Dude, do you even check your LINE? I literally did."

I unlocked my phone and checked the icon. Sure enough, it had the little bubble on it.

"Sorry, I totally missed that. Why didn't you email me to let me know to check it?"

"Uh, because the app tells you? In your notifications?"

"My notifications? Oh. This."

It was not, in fact, just for telling you when your stamina was back in your mobile game of choice. Who knew? You learn something new every day.

I pretended to not be fazed. "Okay, so why are you here anyway?"

At the end of last semester, we had officially become friends. Not the kind to just pop in and hang out at a moment's notice, but here she was anyway. The curry part was irrelevant. Yanami will do as Yanami does.

Having nearly polished off her plate, she was now in the process of scooping up the last of the curry and rice with deft precision. With those final scraps secured in her stomach, she put her hands together in thanks. "Thank you for the food," she said. "Anyway, I'm handing out somen to all my friends."

"Somen?"

I finally noticed the paper bag sitting on the table. Was this one of those mid-year gift things people did sometimes? Did we even have anything to give in return? Maybe a salad oil set. Yanami probably liked oil.

I took a peek. A box just big enough to fit was crammed inside, the words "Value Pack" written on top.

"So not one of those mid-year gift things," I said. "What's this about?"

"A good question. Fantastic, even."

"It was a normal one."

Yanami simply wiped her mouth and didn't acknowledge me. "So basically, this month my dad got paid in noodles."

"He got... What?"

"You heard me. His pay for July is somen. The noodle. A bunch of 'em."

The cicadas got real quiet all of a sudden.

"A whole month's wage is a lot of money," I said.

"We have 300,000 yen's worth of the stuff."

"And it's not, like, code for something, is it? All this is legal?"

"Uh, yeah? You know my family's not the mafia kind, right?" She gazed out the window. I followed suit because why not. "I have had...so much somen."

The August sky—and how blue it was—told of summer's heat, yet the clouds that dotted it betrayed the coming of fall.

"So you're just sharing it around," I said. "Why don't you drop some off to your neighbors?"

"We did. But lately, a bunch of them haven't been answering their doors."

Excommunicado via somen.

"That's unfortunate."

"Yes, it is," she said. A respectful moment of silence passed. "I hope that explains why I've been craving curry."

"Kind of. Yes. Do you want seconds?"

"Already did. I'm good." How silly of me. In a couple of ways, actually. I may have overreacted to what amounted to a friendly somen delivery. "Hey, y'know what? You probably didn't see the LINE this morning either. The lit club's having an emergency meeting."

"Oh, I totally did miss that."

I fumbled around for my phone and checked the club group chat. The president had asked us to meet in the club room tomorrow afternoon. Yanami had already replied, confirming her attendance.

I shot off a quick "will do," then said, "Anyway, don't you have other places to be?"

"You want me gone that badly, huh?" Yanami pouted her lips.

"Only a little. I just figured you had other people to dump somen on."

"Yeah, I have one more—wait, what was that first part?"

"Nothing. I heard the weather's gonna get hotter, so you might wanna get a move on."

New life flared in Yanami's eyes. "After the pears."

"After the what?"

I whipped around. Standing behind me was Kaju, now dressed in her uniform and holding a plate. "I've just peeled these if you'd like some, Yanami-san," she said with an award-winning smile.

"I would! Thanks, Kaju-chan."

I'd forgotten all about her. They'd evidently hit it off. Kaju pattered over like a little puppy and sat down next to me.

"Mmmh, these are good," said Yanami.

"A relative of ours gave them to us—straight from the Kojima orchard," Kaju explained. A sheet of paper and a voice recorder suddenly materialized in her hands. "Now, if it's all right with you, I have a few questions."

She was actually serious about the interview.

"Sure," Yanami agreed. "For homework or something?"

"Yeah...let's go with that! So, firstly, I'll need your date of birth, blood type, at-home relatives, any hobbies or skills, the story of how you two met..."

Kaju was off to the races. I quickly interjected, "Okay, okay, Yanami-san's a very busy girl with a very full schedule. Save that for next time."

"But Oniisama!" she whined. "I haven't heard of any of your exciting school-life escapades yet!"

And she never would.

"Whatever you say. Back to your room now. Go on. Up."

Still grousing and grumbling, Kaju finally marched off. One disaster avoided.

"You make her call you *oniisama*?" Yanami muttered.

"I do not *make* her. Get that fact straight in your head."

"She's really friggin' cute, though. Her face is all round, and her hair is all silky."

"Yeah, people say we look alike."

"People? Like who? Show me them."

They were all busy. Like her. So why was she still here eating?

I dropped my elbows on the table and gave a sideways glance out the window. Puffy cirrocumulus dunes rippled across the sky. How high they soared. Did they hear the cicadas' unending song, I wondered.

"Almost fall," I postulated.

"Pear season, uh-huh. Look, if you wanted some, all you had to do was ask." She pushed the plate toward me, still nibbling on a slice.

"Right. Thanks."

So much for my moment of introspection. I took a pear.

Ten days to the new semester. When those ten days were up, I would look back on this day, on Yanami's coming as the dinosaurs surely did the meteor.

***

Afternoon of the next day, I adjusted my tie as I walked through the gate to Tsuwabuki High School, a conveniently located institution just a short walk from Aidai-Mae Station. A little later, I opened the club room door and joined the only other occupant.

A twig of a girl sat in a folding chair in front of the giant, wall-to-wall bookshelf, reading a book. The curtains, billowing in the wind, obscured her for a moment.

Komari Chika's long bangs and short side ponytail swayed in the breeze. She was a first-year like me, and another true-blue failure heroine like the hungry one before—this time at the hands of none other than our very own president. When we first met last semester, she gave me angry hamster vibes—if a hamster could write mean things on a smartphone. Since then, all mean things came out of her mouth rather than from her phone. We'd made a lot of progress.

Whoever said *I* was unsociable clearly hadn't met Komari Chika.

"Hey, Komari. Been a while."

A strangled noise wrenched out of her mouth. She scrambled for her phone. At light speed, she typed, "You're early. Read or something until it's time."

"Uh, sure." She returned to her book. Welp, back to square one. Weren't mobile games supposed to reward you for logging back in, and not, well, whatever this was? "Hey, so—"

Another choking noise, another reach for her phone.

I waved my hand. "Never mind." I found a chair across the room.

The déjà vu was unreal. I did what I could to fiddle with my phone and ignore the obvious awkwardness, but it was just so much. Even for me, of all people. Every now and then, I tossed her the occasional comment that put no pressure on her to reply. You couldn't rush these things. Had to keep things light. Talk about cute animals and such. In time, her heart would open.

"C-can we please stop talking about rodents?" After twenty minutes, she couldn't take it anymore, flinging the doors to her heart wide open.

"Hey, we were just getting into the nitty gritty of the differences between Mongolian gerbils and hamsters."

"I-I'll google it. Please stop."

Foiled again by the keeper of knowledge. Oh well. My mission was only to broach conversation, and I'd succeeded in that.

I returned to my phone, satisfied, when the (actual) door flung open. Yanami stood at the entrance, leg up against the door on account of her arms being preoccupied with a big cardboard box.

"Heya! You guys are early," she said. I got up and took the box from her and set it on the table. "Thanks. I see the senpai duo isn't here yet."

She plopped down in a chair, her arms hanging tiredly. Komari mumbled something to herself and scooched her chair into a far corner.

"Man, that's heavy," I groaned. "Ah. Somen."

"Sharing is caring, don'tcha know. Take some with you, Komari-chan."

The creature nodded wordlessly from the security of her cove.

Yanami sidled to my side. I leaned away. "Hey, what's her deal?" she asked. "You pull on her hair thingy or something?"

"Why would I?" I grumbled back. "She's just gonna be jumpy for a bit. No shouting and no sudden movements until she acclimates."

"Like a cat café. Gotcha."

A cat café was probably cuter than this.

We left her in peace and quiet, until a few minutes past our scheduled time when the third-years—President Tamaki Shintarou and Vice President Tsukinoki Koto—finally arrived. Right about now, the newlyweds were probably caught between a rock and a soft place, what with college coming up and having just started dating back in July.

"Sorry for the wait," Prez said.

"And for butting into your summer break," Tsukinoki-senpai added.

The two took their seats, much to Komari's relief. She scooted closer.

"Feels like it's been a long time, huh?" I said.

The president shrugged. "These exams we're studying for are rough. I'm at least keeping my head above water." He shot Tsukinoki-senpai a look that she did not return.

"I'm trying, okay? The entrance exams'll happen when they happen," Senpai grouched. "No point rushing, I say."

"The exams aren't going anywhere, but your chances of passing them sure will."

"It's no biggie. I've got a sweet deal lined up in your kitchen if I drop the ball." Tsukinoki-senpai exchanged glances with Komari, who she then shared a meaningfully broad sneer with. The president's face landed firmly in his palm.

Rest assured, the dynamic duo was functioning as normal, for better or worse. Prez had his work cut out for him.

Yanami raised her hand, mercifully pulling the plug on the entire situation. "So what're we doing here?"

"Right, yeah." The president was grateful. "The student council dropped us a line that, starting this year, all clubs are supposed to submit a report on their activity over the summer. I wanted to get you guys' input on that."

That would be a difficult report to make, given we were past Obon already. Along with most of the summer.

"Why are they dropping that on us just now?" I asked.

Prez glanced askance at Tsukinoki-senpai. "They didn't. Apparently, they told us all the way back in July."

"Don't look at me like that," Senpai snapped. "I've been busy studying and getting my license, so it slipped my mind." She held out a piece of paper and waved it around like she was taunting its progenitors.

I didn't bother asking how she had time to go to driver's ed. Had a feeling the president had been asking that same question long enough.

Yanami took the paper. "This says club trips count. What about that one we went on to the beach?"

"We did that before the break," Prez said. "We were a week too early."

Only one other thing came to mind. "We've been uploading our writing online. Does that count?" I asked.

"That's no different from our everyday activity. They want something unique and special that we did over the vacation. So—" He cued in Tsukinoki-senpai.

She produced an A4-size pamphlet from her bag. "We made this sample for a club journal with all our work printed inside. All we need to do is slap on a cover and a colophon, and voilà. It'll look pretty legit."

I flipped through it and found the rom-com I'd been writing. "Lotta empty pages."

"It's just a sample," said Prez. "The final product'll have commentary or articles or something in between all your stuff, is what I'm thinking. Make it seem a little more involved than just copy-pasting our old work."

"Hey, mine's in there too," Yanami pointed out, peeking over my shoulder.

"I want everyone to think about which of your stories you want to see in the final thing," Prez continued. "Or feel free to write something totally new."

"Wh-what are you doing?" Komari asked.

The president twisted his lips. "Don't really have time to put anything down proper right now, so I'll probably just submit a digest of my ongoing series. That goes for you guys too. Don't stretch yourselves thin."

I noticed Tsukinoki-senpai busily scribbling something in a notebook. "What're you doing, Senpai?"

"Shintarou says what I wrote 'isn't fit for publishing,'" she said. "So I'm working on the cover art."

The draft depicted pencil outlines of what would surely become two men. The red flags were looking especially vibrant today.

I pulled up my profile on *Bungou ni Narou* while I considered what to submit. My personal project was a serialized rom-com called *Halfway Down Love Street*, and I was five chapters in. Chapter one made the most sense for a published sample, of course.

I checked my numbers. Still four bookmarks. Exactly the number of people in the room right now, and that was no coincidence.

Only mildly aggrieved by this, I couldn't help but notice a distinct lack of the one club member who had forsaken me—Yakishio Lemon. Sun-kissed track star, lit club artist extraordinaire, and catastrophe heroine number three.

"Hey, Prez, where's Yakishio today?" I asked.

"She said she was busy. I'll pass the info along."

Track was her bread and butter. She did leave her crap lying around sometimes, though, so I assumed she hadn't forgotten about us entirely.

We all were quietly contemplating our works and which to go with, when Yanami blurted, "Okay, I think I'm gonna write a sequel to my first story! What're you gonna do, Komari-chan?"

Komari *er*'d and *um*'d for a bit before finding her phone. "I'm going to write a short story," it read.

"Oooh, nice. Nukumizu-kun?"

"Might proofread chapter one of my series and throw that up," I said.

The president nodded and clapped. "Great. We've all got our tasks. Send me your stuff when you're done." He stood, Tsukinoki-senpai following suit.

"You guys're leaving already?"

Prez snatched Tsukinoki-senpai by the arm. "Gotta make sure Koto doesn't procrastinate on her studying. Catch you guys later."

"Bye! And good luck!" Tsukinoki-senpai got all the way to the door before turning back around. "Oh! Also, would anyone mind standing in for me at the library tomorrow?"

"The library?" I repeated. "What for?"

"Remember when I said we've got connections there? I'm on the committee this year, but I've just been so busy. They don't need much. Just a little help organizing their collection, so I stop by to help on occasion."

Prez popped in over her shoulder. "We get to make requests on new arrivals, plus we get a discount if we buy books through them. It's a give-and-take."

Komari nodded and slowly raised her hand. "I-I can go."

"I can too," I offered.

"Really? That'd be amazing. The more the better," Senpai said. "Gotta stay in the bibliophiles' good books."

Yanami put her hands together in apology. "Sorry, I've got a class reunion thing tomorrow."

"No worries. I know it's sudden. I'll send you guys the specifics later." Senpai waved and left with the Prez, this time for real.

As soon as their voices could no longer be heard down the hall, Komari thumped her book shut and scurried out of the room almost immediately, muttering something under her breath. Probably some form of "goodbye" or "see you later."

Yanami tried and failed to stifle a yawn. Stretched. "Guess I'll head out too. Got me an appointment at the salon for tomorrow."

"Right, the class reunion," I said. "So does that mean Hakamada's gonna be there too?"

"Of course. I mean, 'class reunion' makes it sound bigger than it is. It's just me, Sousuke, and a few old friends going out to catch up a bit."

"Hm. Sounds fun." I didn't exactly sound convincing.

A great, big smile spread across her face. "Karen's gonna be there too."

"Wait, huh? She is?"

Himemiya Karen was our class's local transfer student who came in around May. A total knockout who, in just two months, had gone and swiped Yanami's childhood-friend-slash-crush right out from under her. Yanami certainly had her charms, but her grace and Heroineness simply hadn't been enough to tie Hakamada Sousuke down. Also, Himemiya had bigger "personalities."

"She's a transfer student," I said. "I thought it was a class *reunion*."

"It's an optional 'bring your boyfriend or girlfriend' sorta deal. For introductions."

That made sense enough. What I couldn't get out of my mind was the implication. These would be people from junior high who knew about her and Hakamada's history. And Hakamada would be rolling up with a girl who wasn't Yanami.

She seemed to notice the concern on my face. "Hey, relax. I've changed since last semester. From now on, I'm optimistic, gratitude-giving, happiness-spreading Yanami."

"You don't say."

My expectations were whatever the antonym of "astronomical" would be.

"Lemme make this easier to understand," she said, folding her hands together condescendingly.

"That'd be a first."

"Sousuke and Karen are my best friends. Therefore, their happiness is my happiness. Get it?" I nodded because she expected me to. Yanami approved of this and continued, "So by them going out together and being happy, they've made me happy. I'm grateful beyond words."

"Whatever works for you."

I had my suspicions about this sudden and drastic change of heart. And wouldn't you know it, just then Yanami pulled out a book titled *108 Ways to Phrase a Better You.*

"Whatcha got there?" I asked.

"Uh, 'You are worthy of love exactly as you are. A skewer is a skewer because of the stick...' Hey, you wanna borrow this?"

I understood completely.

Yanami beamed. I shook my head wordlessly.

***

I took my time on my way home, first stopping by the courtyard vending machine. Before I could decide on what to get, a voice came, quiet as a whisper.

It said, "Is someone there?"

I whipped my head around. Not a soul. Must have been my imagination. Sometimes when I got really into a light novel, I could almost hear the characters' voices from the page. Yeah, that was it.

I made my choice of drink.

"You..."

A shrill yelp escaped me, doing a number on my masculinity, as a pale white hand crept around the machine. Had I worn boots, I would have been perfectly justified for shaking in them, thank you very much.

That was when I noticed the scrunchie on the hand's wrist and the gaudy nails. I knew them anywhere.

"Shikiya-senpai?" I called.

From the darkness, it stirred. The thing from the student council. "You're...the literature club boy," she breathed.

Shikiya Yumeko, second-year, leaned heavily against the vending machine. Bright brown, wavy locks rippled over her shoulders. Long and prominent eyelashes shaded her eyes. Most would expect a thick tan to accompany her fashion sense, but her skin was sheet white. She was a gyaru through and through, and I would have been moved by the presence of my favorite archetype if it weren't for the horrifying color-contacts tinting her eyes white and the shroud of darkness she seemed to carry with her.

"What, uh... What're you doing there?" I dared to ask.

"Came for a drink... Got tired. Could you help?" She handed me a coin.

"Um, sure. Just some tea?"

"I LOHAS. Peach... And open it. Please."

So particular. She *was* my senpai, though, so I did as she asked and opened the bottle for her.

"No change," I told her.

"Help me..."

"Sorry?"

Shikiya-san did not elaborate, but from context clues—her closed eyes, her upturned chin, her pale lips hanging open—I picked up on what she was trying to ask for.

"Sh-Shikiya-senpai?"

In any other scenario, those would be the tell-tale signs to go in for a kiss.

I swallowed. Calm. It was an innocent request. I was simply watering my senpai who I barely knew. Anyone could relate.

"Hurry..." She sighed.

"H-hurrying!"

A gentleman didn't keep a lady waiting. I put the rim of the bottle to her lips and tilted it up.

That summer day, in a deserted courtyard, in the shade of a lone vending machine, while the cicadas hissed and buzzed, and a trickle of liquid rolled down Shikiya-san's chin as she gulped, only one question occupied my mind.

What was *actually* happening right now?

"Hey, do you think you can, uh, do it yourself yet?" Shikiya-san's hand suddenly shot up and grabbed mine. I yelped again.

"Too much... Spilling." She took the bottle and stepped out into the sun. "Thanks. Just what the doctor ordered."

The doctor should maybe prescribe a little more, in your case.

I LOHAS sloshed out of the bottle and onto the ground.

"Stop tilting it like that!" I snapped. "Put the cap on first."

I went ahead and did it for her. She then produced a pink, frilly handkerchief and handed it to me. "Wipe, please," she breathily commanded.

"You've literally got it in your hand. Can't you... Oh, forget it."

She reminded me of a three-year-old Kaju. She'd always been well behaved with our parents, but her motor skills reverted a couple of years anytime she ate with me. I basically had to keep a constant eye on her during meals.

"Do your clothes yourself. Got some on your ribbon there." I tried to give the damp cloth back. She didn't take it. "Uh, Senpai? Your handkerchief."

"How is Koto-san...Tsukinoki-senpai?"

"We talked just a while ago. She seems pretty overwhelmed with studying right now."

"I heard she's dating Tamaki-san..." She teetered on her feet. "Is it true?"

"Y-yeah. She is."

"I see..." she mumbled, still wobbling.

I dodged out of the way of her swaying as she shuffled back toward the building. Once I saw she'd made it inside, I let out a sigh. Her relationship to the president puzzled me for a while before I realized something.

"Oops. She never took her handkerchief back."

I considered going after her. And then thought better of it. She wasn't one you confronted without prior preparation. I'd get it back to her later. Somehow. Preferably through the mail or something.

***

The next afternoon, I entered the Tsuwabuki school library. Behind the counter was a girl on the committee, too busy with her laptop to notice me.

I hesitated for a beat, then said, "Um, excuse me."

"Sorry, we're closed. Organizing the shelves today."

"Oh, um, that's why I'm here. To help with that. I'm Nukumizu. With the literature club."

The girl stopped typing and looked up. Her face was long and slender, her complexion fair. She had one singular braid laid over the front of her shoulder.

"Excuse me, then. Koto-senpai mentioned you'd be coming." She held her hands in front of her long skirt and stood. As she came around the counter, I noted the badge on her sleeve denoting her as a second-year. "It's greatly appreciated. We're always short-handed around summer break. Come with me, please."

"Sure thing."

I caught a better look of her when she walked past me. She was willowy, and the features on her face were subtle, unpronounced. An understated kind of cute. The absolute quintessential library and/or lit club aesthetic. Her type seemed to exude melancholy out of every single pore, like a tragic romance wasn't too far off in her future.

We proceeded further into the library. She looked back and gave a mild smile. "I see the lit club is still getting new members. That's a relief."

"Well, technically I've been one for a while. Just recently showing my face more."

"I hope you continue to do so. The other girl is already here and could use some help." A pale finger pointed me to the 900 shelf. The literature section.

Hunched over in the shade of the bookshelves was Komari, muttering to herself and peering at book labels.

"Hey. Sorry I'm late," I said.

She glared, unimpressed, at me through her bangs. "I-I'm sure you are. Y-you take the bottom half of the list."

"Will do. Shouldn't take too long." I grabbed the list and started down the line, reordering volumes according to their label, checking for anything missing.

It quickly got tedious. It was, in fact, taking kinda long. I could feel the yawns coming on already.

"By the way," I broke the silence, "you said you were writing a short story for the journal, right? Any ideas?"

"Y-yeah," Komari replied, which was a surprise. I'd half expected her to go for my throat, as per usual, but now I had a comrade in the battle against drowsiness. "Well, I...actually already wrote it. It's an...i-isekai romance."

What? How? I had barely even started editing chapter one of my thing.

"You work fast. Gonna upload it to *Narou*?"

"Already did l-last night." She fought against a smile trying to form on her lips.

"I take it there's more."

"I-I made the...daily rankings."

"Wow, no kidding? You said it was an isekai romance?"

I took out my phone, and after fiddling around for the genre-specific rankings, clicked a few things. The best works, the chosen works, stood at the top, a league of their own. A few swipes down, I saw a familiar author by the name of "Kuon Usagi."

"So that's your pen name," I said. "Wait, you're in the top ten? You're number *eight*?!"

Komari giggled. "M-my points go up every time I refresh."

Unable to contain her excitement any longer, she hopped up in the air like a rabbit. Usagi indeed.

Narou's daily ranking only went up to 300. Making it at all was an achievement. To make the *top ten* was a miracle among miracles.

"Jesus, yeah, you've got over 3,000 points now," I said.

Her original series was a supernatural, ayakashi sort of deal, which was a niche genre with low point potential. On top of that, she was brand new to the site. And she'd hit the *thousands* overnight. She was up to something. She didn't make it apparent, but I could feel the lording about to begin. It may have only been one short story, but three-k points were three-k points. Forget rabbit, rooster sounded more apt with the levels of cocky she was sure to reach after this.

I dared to sneak a peek at her, and to no surprise, she had the word "smug" written all over her face.

"I-I mean, I'm not in it for the points a-anyway," she swaggered.

"You really think I'm going to forget the way you crapped on my series?"

"Wh-what's important is following your passion. Give it some time, N-Nukumizu."

"Wow, I have never felt more condescended to in my life."

How's the view from the top, Komari? Must look awful nice.

So she had literally a hundred times my points! So what? That didn't mean the quality was proportional. I would be the judge of that.

I clicked on her post.

Literature Club Summer Activity Report: Komari Chika—Single and Ready to Mingle!

"Sylvia Luxéd, we are *through*!"

I was stunned silent. Charges had been levied against me for the attempted murder of the baron's daughter, Anne, and for my troubles, my betrothal to Crown Prince Guster was thus annulled. And in my own residence, no less.

We had been best friends since the concept of such a relationship was even conceivable in our young minds. We were to be wed.

His hair was golden and rippling, his eyelashes more prominent than even mine, his eyes as blue as the sky and twice as captivating. Some claimed their bewitching properties to be arcane in nature.

To me, in that moment, they swam only with contempt.

I proffered a hand, vain though I knew it was. "Prince Guster..."

"Save your excuses for the nuns, Sylvia. You have no future now except for one of the cloth."

"Now wait just a minute. The graduation party hasn't even happened yet!"

Prince Guster's jaw dropped.

This was no ordinary world—this was, in fact, an otome game.

In truth, I was once a normal high school girl, until one day when I awoke in the body of the duke's daughter, Sylvia Luxéd—the villainess of my most recent obsession.

Thanks to my careful plotting, we should have been en route to the true ending of the story. Today was meant to be the final chapter, the Royal Academy of Magic's graduation party. There, His Highness was meant to officially cancel our engagement, after which my parents would disown me, and I'd be sent off to an abbey where I'd spend the rest of my days.

"You're supposed to do all of this at the *party*!" I fumed. "It's like you don't even care about all the meticulous planning I put into making sure all the story events triggered in the right order!"

The only witnesses present were attendants. That simply would not do.

"Sylvia, what the devil are you talking about?" The prince stepped back, surely thinking me hysterical.

He was not far from the truth. Sylvia was a fan favorite, even garnering her own spin-off. In it, she—*I*—was supposed to have caught the attention of a rambunctious foreign prince, stricken by my nerve and audacity at the party. He would find my spunk charming, my feistiness a challenge, and together we would find happiness.

None of that could happen under the present circumstances.

"I-it is over, Sylvia. I cannot abide the atrocity you sought to bring upon the Honorable Anne," the prince said. "However, to cause a scene in public would be a blemish on your reputation that I would not have you suffer. This is the last bit of deference I will grant you, given our history."

Deference? He could shove his deference. If he didn't roast me like a pig over an open flame in full view of everyone, I was going to have to get very comfortable at the abbey.

"Very well. Let us go to the party. There, I will insult Anne to her face, whereupon you will rebuke me and revoke our engagement for all to see!"

That would work. It was an inelegant solution, but we could get back on track.

I hiked up my skirt and made for the door.

"S-Sylvia, the engagement has already been revoked." The prince's feeble murmurings died in the air behind me.

I placed a hand on my hip and fixed him in my icy gaze. "Are you a prince or a damned mouse? Quit your mumbling, get your things, and break up with me at that party!"

"B-but I'm trying to tell you—"

I snatched his arm. "We're going! Now! And don't you forget the documents detailing my wicked crimes. Someone bring round the carriage!"

There was no time to lose. The world would know that I'm single, and by the gods was I ready to mingle.

***

Okay, I was convinced. It definitely read like the kind of thing more people would be into than mine. Which was demonstrably true, given I had a whopping zero readers outside the club.

I was waffling over what to rate it when I noticed Komari frowning. "What's up?"

"Y-Yakishio messaged me," she said.

"You two chat?"

They'd hit it off better than I remembered.

"I-I go running with her sometimes."

Now *that* was a surprise. On second thought, maybe not.

"I vaguely recall you asking for her help on the last day of school," I said. "You're still following through on that?"

"Y-your fault, for the record."

"Sure was. I apologize."

I really did mean it. Just before summer break, Komari had used running as a clever excuse to lure Yakishio away so Yanami and I could talk in private. It never occurred to me that she'd still be trapped doing it.

"You could tell her no," I suggested.

Yanami fidgeted and looked down. "I-I don't really...know how to do that. When people get aggressive."

Wait a minute, you could work that angle into a smut manga.

"Tell me more. Actually, don't. Forget that," I said. "I can always talk to Yakishio for you if you want."

"Go take a nap on the highway..." I may have gotten a bit carried away for a moment there, but that was just plain mean. "A-and it's not *so* bad. She s-slows down for me, and she gave me shoes. A-and she carries me when I get tired." Komari twiddled her thumbs. Yakishio did have a big heart, if nothing else. I felt a little less guilty. "W-waking up at six is...not fun, though."

On that, we agreed.

"At least they say being up early's good for you. I think. I could probably find a research paper that says that."

"Y-you're just saying crap now."

"That I am."

I resumed checking the M section on my current shelf. The sooner we finished, the better.

Some time later, Komari suddenly asked out of the blue, "D-do you know if Yakishio has any siblings?"

"Uh, not that I'm aware of. She might've mentioned a younger sister at one point, but don't quote me on that."

"H-have you seen her around town at all? With a-another person maybe?"

I shook my head. What in the world was she getting at? "Why? Is it important?"

"N-no. Never mind."

I got the feeling she wasn't telling me something, but it would be rude to pry. Also, I didn't feel like it.

I stretched my aching back and got back to work.

***

Two hours trickled by. I finished up, parted ways with Komari, and made for the club room. As much as I craved the comfort of my own home, I needed a quick breather first.

I was walking down the hall that connected to the west annex when a hand patted me on the shoulder. "Hey, Nukumizu. Club today?"

It was Ayano Mitsuki, an old cram school classmate back when we went to junior high together. Perhaps more prominently, though, he was Yakishio's crush. The glasses on his face most certainly spoke to his grades, and he was tall and handsome to boot. One of his current cram schoolmates, Asagumo Chihaya, had had the honor of relegating Yakishio to loser status.

For some reason, he'd randomly come up and chat with me. A strange one, all right.

"Helping out at the library," I said. "You? Weird time to be at school."

It was almost four. Most had a laundry list of other places they'd rather be than on campus that late during summer break.

"You know how it is. Hey, do you know if there's anyone in the club room? I wanted to return that book I borrowed."

"I'm headed there now. I can take it if you want."

"I'd appreciate that." He held it out for me. On his wrist, I noticed an ornate bracelet that looked anything but his style. "Oh. This thing. Bit much, isn't it?"

"Uh, I guess."

I didn't actually care, but he looked like he was dying to tell someone about it. I humored him, as functioning members of society often did for their fellow man.

"Chihaya gave it to me as a gift and told me to never take it off," he said all bashfully. "Silly, I know. It was a surprise and all, so what can you do, right?"

He looked positively *downtrodden*. I'd been hanging around the losing team for so long that it nearly went right over my head that I was witnessing the classic "girlfriend humblebrag."

He didn't stop talking, and I didn't stop nodding.

***

I reached the club room a ways down the hall and tried the door. Either Komari had gotten there first or someone had forgotten to lock it, because it was slightly ajar.

I entered.

"Oh, Nukkun! Hey!"

I slammed the door back shut. It was not Komari. It was Yakishio Lemon. Correction: half-naked Yakishio Lemon.

"You're supposed to *shut* the door when you're changing!" I shouted through it.

"Who peed in your cereal this morning?" said Yakishio as she sauntered out, still buttoning her blouse.

"What is it with you and constantly getting naked in front of people?!"

"Oh, whatever. I'm wearing stuff underneath," she said offhandedly. "I'm more covered up than when I'm on the track, even." She looked up and cocked her head. "Wait, what do you mean 'constantly'?"

Shoot. Right. She didn't remember that little debacle in the storage shed.

"Nothing," I said. "The hallway is not for changing."

I shoved her through the door, ignoring her appalled "Hey!" Then swung it shut. Safe.

"You're such a prude, Nukkun. Shove this in that bag over there."

A towel came flying at me. Deliberately ignoring the sweaty clothes wrapped up inside it, I did as she said and stuffed it into her duffel bag.

Wait, why was I in the room with her?

I found myself a seat and stayed there, exceptionally still, though not out of peace of mind. I stole a glance. She sure was still changing without a care for my presence. Only once her blouse was completely on did I fully let my guard down. Ah, so *that* was how those ribbons went on.

"Why are you changing in here anyway?" I asked.

"The track team's room is too small. First-years don't get dibs, so I just come here when I'm in a hurry." Yakishio adjusted one of her ribbons in the mirror. "What're *you* doing here? It's summer break."

"Came to help out at the library. Hey, you forgot something." She had left her trademark lemon hair clip sitting on the table.

She picked it up and looked at it funny. "Weird. I thought I put it in my bag."

"Must've taken it off for practice."

"I usually never do, but I just had it polished. Felt bad getting it all dirty again the day after."

Couldn't judge a book by its cover (or in this case, its contents). Despite Yakishio's Yakishioness, she *was* still one of prettiest girls in school. Appearances did matter to her.

She clipped on the hair lemon and fixed it just right. "President Tamaki told me we're making a journal?"

"Yeah, to make it seem like we actually did something over the summer," I said. "I'm just gonna fix up chapter one of my series. What about you?"

"Good question. I like my pictures, but I could also maybe try writing something for a change." She fussed with her bangs, then pumped her fist and went, "Nice," when she was satisfied. She was being awfully finicky.

Yakishio's phone blipped. She checked it, read whatever it was, and smiled.

"What's up?" I asked.

"Nothin'. Gotta go. See ya!"

"Your socks are laying over there," I called after her.

"No biggie!" she called back. And without another word, she skipped away.

"Somewhat of a biggie," I grumbled. I carefully picked them up with a handkerchief and tossed them in her bag, which she had also left behind.

Peace at last. I fished for that book I'd been reading and flipped it open, but my eyes soon started to glaze over. I closed it and stared up at the ceiling.

A deserted building on summer break. A guy and a girl who had *almost* been a thing.

I shook my head and opened my book again. I was thinking too much.

***

Rubbing the sleep from my eyes, I stumbled into the living room.

"Good morning, Oniisama!" Kaju said the moment I trudged in. An apron hung from her neck. She pulled a chair out for me, beaming. "Breakfast is ready!"

"Morning," I said. "Mom and Dad already left for work?"

"Oniisama, it's nine. They're long gone."

Time had gotten away from me last night while I worked on my journal submission, and as a result, I must've had a later start than I thought.

Kaju giggled and set a plate of pancakes in front of me. "I'm trying something new this morning. I hope they turned out okay." She topped them with something sweet-smelling. "I mixed in rice flour, and this here's a white peach compote. Have as much as you like." A bit of the compote trickled onto her finger, which she promptly licked off. "It's sweet with a tangy undertone. You'll like it! Oh, and I made lemonade too. Eat up!"

Lightly dusted with powdered sugar and even garnished with a fancy mint leaf, these pancakes looked straight out of a fancy breakfast joint.

"Thanks. Looks great." I grabbed a knife and fork and was about to dig in when I noticed the untouched plate next to me. "You haven't eaten yet?" I asked.

"Ah, silly me!" Kaju bonked herself on the head with a goofy smile. "I was so caught up in the kitchen that I completely forgot."

What a cute little goober, I thought. Preparing such a feast and somehow forgetting her own plate.

I made to nudge her plate to the chair opposite me, but she sat down next to me before I could. "Shall we dig in, Oniisama?"

"Sounds good to me."

My knife glided through the fluffy stack and thus began another peaceful breakfast.

Kaju raised an eyebrow at me. "You've been to school two days in a row. Have things been busy?"

"Club's kept me a little preoccupied. Dunno if 'busy' is the right word."

I didn't have much for a point of reference. Most of the time I wasn't doing much of anything.

"I'm so happy for you," Kaju said. "That new friend of yours is the girl who visited recently, isn't it? Yanami-san, her name was."

I grunted and stuffed my mouth with pancakes.

I'd told her that I'd made a new friend, just not who they were. Partly out of shyness, partly out of prudence.

"You should invite her over yourself next time," she pressed. "We still haven't finished the interview."

Ideally, it would stay that way. I swallowed some lemonade. "It's not that big a deal. We don't even really hang out that much."

"Not in the beginning, sure. Buuut..." Kaju got right up to me, eyes lighting up. "She was *very* pretty! She is the one who will carry on the culinary secrets of the Nukumizu family! I just know it! We'll start with miso soup, then move on to the finer fundamentals of Japanese, Western, and Chinese cuisine, and then we'll—"

There she went again. You had to know when to pump the brakes with that girl.

"Chill," I said. "We're not like that. Not even close."

"But Oniisama, it's only a matter of time. Any member of the fairer sex would find it hard to *not* fall in love with you once she got to really know you. We *must* be prepared!" She gasped suddenly and leaned in. "Unless there's someone else in the literature club who's earned your affection. The tan girl would be lovely, and I'll even retract my previous doubts about the little one on account of the fact that we would be able to share wardrobes, thus becoming fast friends. Gosh, it would be so simple! Anyway, tell me. Tell me! Which one is it?!"

I held my hands up between me and her. "Slow down, Kaju. Count to six with me. Ready? One, two, three..."

"Four, five, six..." She held a hand to her chest and inhaled deeply, regaining composure. I patted her on the head for a job well done. She made a mewing sound and nuzzled my hand.

Now that that was out of the way, I used my free hand to continue eating. While I chewed on my next bite, my phone lit up next to my plate. A notification.

A quick glance made me freeze for a split second.

Yana-chan: You up? Wanna hang out somewhere?

What in the world did Yanami want with me?

Kaju took her chance to slip away and plop herself onto my lap. "Is that Yanami-san? She's asking you out, Oniisama!"

"So it would seem."

"This is huge!" She grinned from ear to ear. "It might as well be a date!"

"We're not like that," I insisted. "She probably just wants to talk about something."

I sighed. What to do.

An invite first thing in the morning, the day after her class reunion. My Yanami Sense was tingling.

Kaju watched me type, *Busy.*

She looked up at me. "Are you sure?"

"Sure I'm sure. She'll find someone else."

Then, like clockwork, my phone rang. The name "Yanami" appeared smack in the middle of the screen. She couldn't take no for an answer.

Kaju squeezed my hand around the phone, smiling. "Go, Oniisama. Friends don't keep friends waiting."

A course of action that would have been made easier were she not sitting on my lap.

***

Three o'clock on the dot. The café by city hall. While I waited on Yanami to show up, I passed the time by people-watching. The place had a rustic vibe, and according to the internet, the hotcakes (very different from pancakes) were a must-have. It was a wonder I'd never been here before with how close it was to home.

"Your iced coffee, sir."

"Oh, thanks," I said.

I eyed the extra glass of water placed across from me. The condensation streaming down it mirrored the metaphorical sweat streaming down my back.

I was at a café with a girl—okay, not right now, but soon enough—during summer vacation.

Kaju's ramblings aside, I couldn't get the date idea out of my head. If the manga and light novels I'd read were to be believed, you could apparently go on these without technically being a couple.

So what did that make this?

The bell on the door jingled as I messed with the milk and creamer cups that had come with my coffee. My head jerked up. It was Yanami. She wore a dark navy blouse and a gray pleated skirt that hung just above her knees. I'd seen her in casual clothes on the trip last month, but this was different. This was her dressing for show.

I became distinctly conscious of my posture all of a sudden. *Was* today a date?

Yanami scanned around, found me, and walked over.

"H-hey." I put on my best smile. "So, um, what made ya wanna hang out?"

She threw herself into the seat, saying nothing, and downed the glass of water in one go, *thunking* it back down on the table a little too hard. "Burn it," she growled. "Burn it all down."

I wondered what could have possibly gotten her goat. "What happened at the class reunion?"

She flinched at the words "class reunion."

"I shouldn't be surprised," she said. "I'm not, really. I just thought I was ready. But actually seeing it. Up close. It's not the same. It defies all logic."

This was most definitely not a date. At least I could stop being all nervous.

I leaned back. "Were they, like, all flirty or something?"

"That's whatever. I got over that month one. They could play the 'I love you more' game all day in front of me and I wouldn't even gag at this point." She dropped an elbow on the table, her cheek resting in her hand as she lazily browsed the menu. "Not like PDA's their style anyway."

"Well, that's good."

"It's irrelevant. I don't care about that. It's the way they eat, the way they throw out each other's trash, the way they carry stuff for each other. It's like they share a brain." Yanami shook her head wearily. "They talk without needing to use words. They share point cards. They have the same ringtone. They coordinate little accessories. When it's time to split, they walk home together like they're going to the same place. Like it's nothin' at all." She stole my water and downed that too. *Thunked* it again. "It's like they zoomed straight past the honeymoon phase and they're *married* already! Like, hello?! How far are they gonna go in a friggin' month?!"

I'd say they'd gone about as far as one could in that time frame, personally.

While Yanami caught her breath, I asked for more water. "Oh, and a new glass, please."

"What? I got cooties or something?" Yanami griped.

It was a me thing. I didn't do eating or drinking after others had already had their mouths on it.

"Gonna order anything?" I asked.

"Yeah, sure, ignore me," she grumbled. "I'll just have a, uh, cream soda."

"Wow. No hotcakes?"

I'd kind of assumed she chose this place specifically so she could stuff her face with the stuff.

Yanami waited for the waiter to leave. "Nukumizu-kun," she said grimly. "Let me tell you a secret. Somen. Are. Carbs." True. "They may be cold and noodly, but do not be deceived like I was. You look at them, and it's just a few gluteny strings, yeah? Surely, they're not *that* bad. How does anyone gain weight off of *those* little guys?"

"So basically, you had too much somen and—"

"No!" she snapped. "Whatever you're about to say, no! I did not!"

"You are aware cream soda has carbs, right? Like, a lot actually."

"Drinks don't count. Ice cream too, actually, according to some people."

I took it that "some people" meant Yanami and Yanami alone.

Our waiter returned with her cream soda. It was your standard melon green with a scoop of vanilla ice cream on top. Yanami pointed her phone at it.

"So you're a picture taker," I said.

"It's for Instagram. *Dang*, I'm good at photos."

Wasn't that that one social media site where people post pictures? My only impression of it came from the amount of food people wasted by ordering fancy-looking junk just for likes and then not finishing it. That had been a controversy for a hot minute, but I sincerely doubted it concerned Yanami in the slightest.

She tapped at her phone a bit, then showed it to me. "Look, see? I better be in your likes later."

"I don't have an account. And isn't that my hand in the corner there?"

Off to the side of the colorful, bubbly soda was none other than me. Not the kind of collab people probably wanted.

"Huh. You're right," said Yanami. "Man, your fingers are bony. You eating enough?"

"Plenty, and you should probably retake that."

"Too late. Already uploaded it." She continued to fiddle with her phone while she chipped away at the ice cream. Then, an idea flitted across her expression. "I just made bait."

"You made what?"

Yanami cracked a smirk, crossed her legs, and flipped her hair all in one motion. "Oh, my sweet summer child. I'm going fishing."

"I'm still confused."

"There is a portion of Instagram that likes to drop hints—bait, if you will—that they're spending time with the opposite sex. Sometimes it's to subtly brag about a significant other or make people think you're taken."

"Oh. I've heard of famous people getting flamed for stuff like that." Incidentally, many of my favorite voice actresses just so happened to all have brothers. And suspiciously close in age, at that. "But, I mean, you're just some girl."

"Check it out, though. My friends are eating it up." She held her phone out to me again. "They're all dying to know who you are. Look at them going crazy. Man, I'm a genius."

"Just one question about all this," I said. "Why?"

Yanami gave me a deadpan look. "Think about whether you really want me to answer that."

"Right. Sorry."

"You should be. Oh, Kasumi-chan! I haven't seen her in forever." She grinned and scrolled for a while before suddenly freezing up.

"Something wrong?"

"You know, ever since the reunion, a lot of guys I used to know from junior high have been reaching out to me. Like, a lot of 'em. All at once."

"Okay...?"

"I'm serious. My DMs are literally blowing up. God, I'm so popular it's scary."

"I'm so happy for you."

I could think of nothing else to say, and so I sipped my iced coffee (now sans ice) instead. Yanami went to town on her slowly melting ice cream, occasionally shooting glances my way like she wasn't done talking.

"So are you, like, in the market for a boyfriend then?" I reluctantly asked in an effort to appease her.

Yanami pretended to think about it, rolling her spoon between her fingers. "Nah, don't think so. Just not looking for that sorta thing right now."

"Pray tell."

"Girls'll start trying to introduce me to friends left and right, guys'll be asking me out pretty much twenty-four-seven, and it's like I literally *just*... Wait."

"What?"

"The guys asking me out now. Something just hit me. Dude, even Tanaka's in here." She scrolled and scrolled, frowning and making faces, then her jaw dropped. She looked up at me. "Do these people think I'm easy?! They're totally just trying to be my rebound, aren't they?!"

"That is one likely interpretation, yes." She had to realize it sooner or later. If only she could have lived in blissful ignorance a while longer. I added some creamer to my coffee in somber solidarity. "But hey, there's probably at least one or two in there who actually care about you as a person."

"I actually can't tell if you're genuinely trying to cheer me up, but I want you to know it's not working," she said flatly. "Anyway, whatever. I think I'm just done with guys for now." I wondered what that made me. Yanami splashed around her soda bitterly with her spoon. "I'm outta ice cream..."

"A travesty."

As my eyes wandered out the window, I found them attracted toward a magnetic someone. A girl in a Tsuwabuki uniform, complete with those four idiosyncratic ribbons, skipped by. A lemon clip adorned her short hair, her skin a tawny brown.

"Hey, it's Yakishio," I said.

"Lemon-chan?" Yanami peered over, using her spoon to bail puddles of soda into her mouth.

"What's she doing in her uniform?"

Yanami gasped. "Nukumizu-kun! Down!" She snatched my head and whacked it into the table.

"Ow!" I howled. "What the hell are you doing?!"

"Keep your head down! She'll see us!"

"Why do we care if Yakishio—"

That was when I saw she wasn't alone. Ayano Mitsuki walked beside her—her crush. Yakishio was so obviously starstruck, the way she bounced at his side.

"What're they doing together?" I mumbled. Hadn't she moved on after it came out that Ayano was taken?

Yanami hid behind her glass of soda until they passed, then craned her neck to watch as they left. When they were out of sight, she slowly sat up straight.

"I got bad vibes from that, Nukumizu-kun," she said. "No guy with a girlfriend goes out on the town with another girl on *summer break* of all times. I smell infidelity."

"Come on, they're old friends. Would it be cheating if, say, you and Hakamada hung out alone together?"

"Yes. A hundred percent."

"All right, well, you got me there."

Them's the breaks. They had chosen their path, and as third-party observers, our only recourse was to let them walk it.

Yanami turned her soda up, gulped it down, wiped her mouth with a handkerchief, and thunked the glass on the table for a third time. "Hurry and finish! We gotta go!"

"Go where?"

"After them!" she enunciated impatiently.

Yanami jumped up. Impulsive curiosity shimmered in her eyes.

"You go do that," I said. "I'm not interested."

"What?"

I added some milk to my coffee. Waiting until it was half gone to do that made it sorta like a café au lait. Yanami stared at me, expressionless, while I took a slow, savoring sip.

She tapped the receipt on the table. "I can just not pay this, you know."

"Dude."

Motivated partly by fear, mostly by annoyance, I chugged the last of my coffee. I got up, but not without a sigh that I was sure she could hear.

***

Yanami and I scanned the street upon exiting the café. Neither Yakishio nor Ayano were anywhere to be found.

"Guess they're gone," I said. I waved to Yanami. "That's that then. Later."

"Seriously?!" She got a lock on my arm before I could get far. "We haven't even *tried* looking for them!"

"I mean, do *you* see them anywhere? And we're not private eyes. You really expect us to be able to tail them like we're in a movie? In real life, they call those stalkers, and people call the police on them..."

I trailed off, not for lack of confidence but more incredulity. Because there, around the corner of the café we'd just come out of, was a dyed-in-the wool stalker. They had long hair parted straight at the middle of their forehead. They were short, probably a girl. She wore sunglasses and a face mask. Four ribbons lined her blouse. A Tsuwabuki student.

A glance one way, a glance another, and she scurried out from her hiding place and toward us. She stopped to slip something that looked like chocolate underneath her mask and nibbled on it.

Why did she look so familiar?

"You're right," Yanami muttered. "I *would* call that a stalker."

"I rest my case."

The girl came up close, pulled out some weird, antiquated cell phone-esque device with an antenna, and held it over her head.

"D'you know her?" Yanami asked me.

"Even if I did, not anymore. Let's get outta here before she implicates us in something."

"She's starin' at you pretty hard."

"Please be lying."

Against my better judgment, I slowly turned to check. Sure enough, she was looking straight at me.

She pitter-pattered right on over. "Hello, Nukumizu-san," she said, prying apart her sunglasses and mask. "Do you remember me?"

Big, round eyes peered up at me.

"Oh," I said. "I guess I do."

As unfortunate as that was. The stalker's identity was none other than Ayano Mitsuki's girlfriend, Asagumo Chihaya. She was about as short as they came, though surprisingly well proportioned and with a particularly small face. She had the look and posture of a ballerina.

"You're Asagumo-san," I continued. "I think we met in cram school but never really talked."

"I don't recall us speaking either," she said. "It's nice to re-meet you." She replaced her sunglasses and mask and lowered her head. From the parting of her bangs, the sun gleamed off her forehead.

"Right, um, likewise."

"To that point, have either of you seen Mitsuki-san or Yakishio-san around here?"

"Actually..." Yanami started to say.

I shot her a look and shook my head. "N-nope. Can't say we have."

"I see. I could have sworn they'd be here." Asagumo-san stood on her tiptoes and held the device up. "The signal here is just awful. I'll have to get more creative."

Yanami ogled the antenna'd thing above her.

"Well, we'd better get going," I said. "Right, Yanami-san?"

"Hey, uh, what's-your-name. Asagumo-san?" she chimed in. "What do you mean 'signal'? What's that thingy for?"

"Yanami-san!" I hissed.

"What? I'm curious."

Asagumo-san narrowed her eyes at us. "You *have* seen Mitsuki-san, haven't you?"

She produced a black, palm-sized rod. A red light glowed at one end.

"What is *that*?" I asked.

"An important device. See the red light?"

I did, but it wasn't like it made any difference. The significance of the red light still eluded me.

Asagumo-san flicked her head. "Let's take this somewhere else, shall we?"

***

We did indeed take it somewhere else. That much I agreed to. My issue came from where that "somewhere" ended up being.

"Did we have to pick my room? We were literally right in front of a café."

No one cared. Yanami couldn't stop pacing around, scrutinizing every little thing I owned. "We were just at that café," she said. "Whoa, this poster's made of fabric?"

"Yanami-san, it's rude to stare in a boy's room. You're supposed to pretend you don't see anything," In came Asagumo-san with the assist no one asked for. She sat upright on a cushion on the floor, jotting things known only to her in a notebook.

Yanami prodded my treasure—my B2 *Masou Senki Shinonome* tapestry. "Is it bad if I don't?"

"I mean, not really," I said. "I'm not embarrassed or anything."

"Yanami-san, you're nearing a very dangerous line," Asagumo-san interjected. "Otaku are very particular about the way their paraphernalia are appreciated, and they take exceptional umbrage if you don't do so with proper respect. Also, if a girl I knew came into my room and wouldn't take her eyes off the underwear-clad women on my wall, personally I would crawl into a hole and die."

"Technically, it's not underwear. It's, er, battle gear," I corrected, probably pointlessly. We *had* to move away from this topic.

Yanami disagreed. "They fight in that? Isn't armor supposed to, y'know, cover things?"

"Th-they, uh...emit mana...from their skin," I stammered. "For the, um...Sigma Drive."

"Huh. Is that related to why they're lying in bed together?"

I shut my eyes and rolled my head back. *Jesus Christ, kill me.*

The door clicked open.

"When the Enlightened Five gather, their Sigma Drives harmonize as one, thus unleashing Pashupatastra, the ultimate weapon. Please do not misconstrue their embrace or manner of clothing as anything but purely strategic."

"Kaju." I hadn't read that far yet...

Once she was finished dropping mega spoilers, my sister entered the room proper. "I brought refreshments, Oniisama."

"Thanks. Leave them on the table," I said.

Kaju distributed iced tea to everyone, grinning warmly. "Make yourselves at home." She lowered her head to Yanami, who had darted over the moment she'd heard "refreshments." "Yanami-san," she said. "I apologize for the lapse in our hospitality during your last visit."

"Oh. No, it's fine," Yanami replied, visibly deflated at the lack of snacks.

Asagumo-san bowed politely at Kaju. "So sorry for barging in. I promise I won't stay long."

"Please, take your time," Kaju insisted. "I believe I missed your name."

"Asagumo. Kazuhiko-san and I go to the same school."

Kaju's face, smile and all, stiffened like ice. "'*Kazuhiko*-san'?"

"Whoa, you just went crazy pale," I said. "You okay?"

"Oniisama. May I inquire as to the nature of your relationship with our fine guest here?"

"What she said. We go to the same school. She has a boyfriend."

"Scandalous," my sister muttered under her breath.

"I heard that," I snapped. "Stop being rude and go back to your room. The grown-ups have things to talk about."

"As you wish, Oniisama." With surprisingly little resistance, she was gone.

Asagumo-san blinked her big, round eyes. "I figured I should use your first name since she was also a Nukumizu-san. Did I touch a nerve?"

Little bit, but we'd cross that bridge when we came to it.

"Dang, I'm surprised you knew his first name. I sure didn't," Yanami said, sipping on her tea with all the blissful ignorance in the world. I really shouldn't have been as surprised as I was.

"I have something of a photographic memory," said Asagumo-san. "In fact, I could recite everything on your bookshelf already."

"I would really rather you didn't. Anyway, didn't you have something to tell us?" I asked.

"Right. Of course." Asagumo-san adjusted her posture and lowered her voice respectfully. "Firstly, I want to thank you for your time. As for what I was doing when we bumped into each other, that will require some explanation."

Surely she hadn't been skulking around for the fun of it. I searched for the straw with my mouth and sipped on my tea.

"I'm just going to put all my cards on the table," she said. "I think Mitsuki-san might be cheating on me. I've been trying to find proof and catch him in the act."

It didn't take a genius to guess with who. I really didn't know what to say. Yakishio was the last person I'd have thought would end up being party to an affair.

Yanami spoke up for me. "What makes you think that? Like, if they're just hanging out, then..." She looked my way. "Lemon-chan's *maybe* the one person I could see that being okay with."

"Even if they're hanging out in secret?"

"Okay, well..." Yanami held her palm up at me.

I tagged myself in. "Now, I'm no expert on relationships, much less romantic ones, but what if he just isn't telling you specifically because he doesn't want you worrying?"

"Very true." Yanami nodded. "The man has a point."

What experience she was drawing from to confirm my theory was anyone's guess.

"Maybe," Asagumo-san admitted. "I do want to trust him, and from what I know of Yakishio-san, I want to believe she's not the kind of person to do something like this."

"That's good. Very big of you," I said. "Well, I think that about wraps things up, don't you?"

"But that's exactly why I need to see for myself why they're going around behind my back," she went on.

The situation unfurled yet again.

"Sure, I get that, but finding out when and where they're meeting isn't something you can just do on a whim."

Today was an insane coincidence. If you lived in the same neighborhood, maybe it could happen, but realistically you'd never bump into them on purpose.

"Today gave me all the data I need," she said. "All I have to do is collate it and I'll triangulate where exactly they're going."

"Data?" Yanami parroted. "You've got data?"

"I do. Long story short, I've already collected and analyzed a good deal of it." Asagumo-san dug through her pocket and fished out a small bag. She popped it open and started munching on a Black Thunder bar with both hands. Yanami's eyes were laser targeted on the thing. "Would you like some?" she offered.

"For real?" Yanami took the bar for herself, then nodded at me. "We can trust her, Nukumizu-kun."

Maybe she *was* easy.

"I can go get you something if you're hungry," I said.

"No need," Asagumo-san refused. "I'm simply replenishing glucose levels. It's what the brain runs on, after all." She pulled out another Black Thunder bar. "You can achieve the same result with pills, but the feminine urge to consume sweet treats is not one that I, personally, am capable of resisting."

"So you like sugar. Got it."

She gave me a look. "It's nothing so base, I'll have you know. Glucose is the basis from which all neurotransmitters are derived and thus is the most straightforward way to stimulate the brain's reward system. My actions are based solely on logic."

"Yup. You're so right. I am totally picking up what you're putting down," Yanami fervently agreed. I could almost see a couple of neurons behind her eyes trying to make a spark.

"I knew someone would. Here. Have some quail sablés."

"Woo! Yay!" The baser of the two took her reward without hesitation.

"Anyway," I said, "I don't like the idea of snooping around Yakishio. She's our clubmate, so if you're looking for backup, it can't be me."

Asagumo-san lowered her eyes sadly. "Right. I suppose neither of you has any reason to want to do that. You wouldn't go spying on an impulse."

"Especially not on an impulse." That earned me a look from Yanami, though not enough to get her to pause on her cookie.

"I'm not out to get her. Really," Asagumo-san said. "I just want to know what I am to Mitsuki-san. What *she* is to him. So I can decide accordingly."

"Decide?" I echoed back.

She nodded staunchly. "I'm well aware that they're old friends. That she most likely thinks that's all they are. And that she wishes they could be more." I gulped. It wasn't news to me, but just hearing it said out loud in this context put me on edge. "I care very much about Mitsuki-san. His happiness is all I want, even if I'm not necessarily a part of it."

Yanami scrunched her eyebrows. "Now hold on a minute, Asagumo-san. Are you saying you'd just *give up* your boyfriend to Lemon-chan? Just like that?"

"I've always felt out of place," said Asagumo-san. "That they might be the better couple, and I'm just the thief who swooped in and stole Mitsuki-san away." Her lips formed a fake smile. "Even that's giving myself too much credit. I knew I didn't belong between them, and I forced myself in anyway."

Neither Yanami nor I knew what to say.

A moment later, a more genuine smile spread across her face. "That's why I want to know how *he* feels. And if he wants to be with Yakishio-san," she straightened up as tall as she could, "I'm prepared to stand aside."

We stayed quiet. Asagumo-san sipped some tea. "I'm too involved," she continued. "I won't be able to judge the situation from an unbiased perspective. That's what I wanted the two of you for."

I felt for her. I really did. But...

"I'm sorry," I said. "I think you'll have to do this on your own. Treating my clubmate like a suspect doesn't feel right to me."

This time, it was Asagumo-san who fell silent. She took out another snack and, after slowly nibbling through the entire thing, pasted on a brave smile. "I understand. It's a problem between the three of us. I'm sorry for trying to make it yours."

"Hey, don't be. I'm sorry we couldn't help."

Even I wasn't entirely convinced with my answer. Something inside gnawed at me, like a crack in my certainty. Something I couldn't place.

Yanami finished up her sablé and, after licking the crumbs off her fingers, quietly said, "I think I wanna help you."

I whipped around to face her. "Yanami-san!"

She grinned placidly at me. "I'm not being impulsive this time, Nukumizu-kun." She turned back to Asagumo-san. "One thing, though, to be clear. I'm Lemon-chan's friend, first and foremost. I'm gonna hear her side on this."

"I understand," Asagumo-san said. "Thank you."

I turned that something over and over in my head while they exchanged contact info.

What was I other than an outsider? If Yakishio got with Ayano, good for them. If Ayano stayed with Asagumo-san, good for them.

The something remained a mystery.

Yanami looked at me. "What's the plan?" she asked. Genuinely. No teasing or goading altered her tone.

The something made my lips move on their own. They said, "Okay. I'll help."

"Thank you both so much." Asagumo-san bowed her head low.

"Okay, but first of all, how are you planning on ambushing them anyway?" I asked. "We can't just follow them around all day."

I had it on good authority (my own testimony) that she was god-awful at tailing people.

"Not to worry," Asagumo-san stated. "Can I proceed under the assumption that you saw Mitsuki-san in front of the café moments before our meeting?" Yanami and I exchanged glances. We nodded. "Then I'll add that to my considerations."

She opened up her notebook and started leafing through the pages. After a lengthy and thorough scan, she thumped it shut and looked up again.

"I've got it. Next time they meet, I'll nail them."

INTERMISSION

It's Never What You Think It'll Be

MOMOZONO JUNIOR HIGH'S CLASS THREE WAS buzzing with second-years, classmates reuniting with classmates. One of them, however, found herself in a less jovial mood.

"Oh, Oniisama," Nukumizu Kaju sighed, gazing wistfully out the window. "How far apart we've grown."

A taller girl came over to her. "What's up, Nuku-chan?"

"Ah. Gon-chan."

Kaju languidly lifted her chin from her hands. Gondou Asami was her closest friend in class, and certainly the tallest and most mature.

"Go on," she urged with gentle concern. "Hit me with whatcha got."

"Do you remember me saying my brother dearest made his first friend?"

"Oh, yeah. You were over the moon 'bout that."

"And I still am. Honest. But this girl—she's so pretty." Kaju slumped over her desk like a ragdoll. "And it's not just her. There's another. Just recently, in fact, he let them both into his room *without* informing me, and it was a veritable war zone!"

"Sounds like the guy's got moves," said her friend. "He handsome or what?"

Kaju lurched up off her desk. "Of course he is! My Oniisama is the most wonderful and—" The fire in her eyes dimmed a little, snuffed by doubt. "You'd best watch yourself. I refuse to call you Oneesan one day."

"Oneesan?" Gon-chan seemed to think this over. "I could get down with a girl like you for a little sister."

"Gon-chan!" Kaju blurted.

"Kidding, kidding! But it's a good thing he's popular, yeah? Doesn't that make you proud?"

"I know, it's just...two? At once? And I haven't even interviewed *either* of them!"

"Just the other day you were chattin' my ear off about how you wanted him to have the best girlfriend in the world."

"It's just not what I thought it'd be," Kaju whined. "I thought that when he promised his heart to someone, I would simply watch fondly from afar while the magic happened, but now he's got one on each arm doing God knows what. Agh, there's tragedy afoot, I just know it!" She collapsed onto her face once more, kicking and flailing her legs.

Gon-chan consoled her with a pat on the head. "There, there. You've always got me as a backup."

"I don't want you, I want Oniisama," she moaned.

"Ouch. Rejected."

Kaju sat back up. "You *are* my best friend, though, just so you know."

"Gosh, you're cute, y'know that? Just marry me already."

"Nuh-uh."

Kaju slumped back to her desk, comforted by Gon-chan's head pats.

How the poor, hapless fourteen-year-old wished she could be happy for her dear, no-longer-friendless Oniisama, and for that to be the end of it. Unfortunately, emotions were complicated. Much unlike the soothing sensations of the comforting head pat.

Too Many Losing Heroines!

LOSS 2

Asagumo Chihaya and the Goose Chase

TWO DAYS AFTER THROWING OUR LOTS IN WITH Asagumo Chihaya, she messaged us both to meet up. As soon as possible.

The rendezvous point: the Kalmia mall at Toyohashi Station, near the north side. I hurried into the station from the outdoor deck. At a glance, I was the first to arrive, so I positioned myself in front of Kalmia while I caught my breath.

The clock just hit half past two. Shoppers thronged in and out. Others waiting for their own people stood with me.

I turned my gaze away from them and to the ground. "What am I doing?" I muttered to myself.

I wasn't in this to expose Yakishio and all of her dark secrets. Something just didn't sit right with me about putting her on trial, so I involved myself. Still, I couldn't shake the feeling that none of this was my business.

Before I knew it, someone had come up next to me. I stole a peek to find that it was a girl in a sailor uniform. She had thick-rimmed glasses, and her hair was done in two loose braids.

Also, she was going to town on a basket of takoyaki. This girl had too many descriptors.

"Wait, Yanami-san, is that you?!" I blurted.

She flashed me a smirk. "Took ya long enough." She pinched the frame around where the glasses part should have been and pushed them up, all smug-like.

"Those don't even have lenses."

"They're for show. Make me look smarter, don't they?"

They didn't, but I nodded anyway. "I have a few questions," I said. "I'll summarize them: What's with the look?"

"Duh, it's a disguise. So they don't notice us. It's actually just my old junior high uniform, but I totally still pull it off, eh?"

"I mean, it's only a year old, so—" I stopped. There were...aspects of the role she was definitely struggling to "fit into," shall we say.

"What? What'd you get all quiet for?" She popped a takoyaki into her mouth.

"Nothing. You do you."

The crew was all here and ready to go, except for the brains of the entire operation who was nowhere to be seen. Yanami called her phone but got no answer.

"I'm surprised you're even here," Yanami said, typing out a DM on LINE. "Thought this sorta thing'd be your kryptonite."

"What do you mean 'this sorta thing'?"

"*This*. The whole 'is Lemon-chan cheating' investigation. Would you have done it if it were *me* asking?"

Probably not, but my sensible side told me not to say that out loud. "What about you? Why are you bothering?"

Yanami stopped typing. "Did you see the way Lemon-chan looked at him when they were together?"

I nodded. It came to me clear as day. The smile she wore, "beaming" didn't do it justice. It was like a bud on the verge of blossoming, and all its feelings with it.

I could read between the lines. Even the densest brick of a man on the planet—even Ayano had to see what everyone else saw.

The uncomfortable thing was the notion that he *did* see it, and he was going along with her anyway. That Yakishio knew that he knew and didn't care.

"You don't look at a guy who's taken like that. You just don't," Yanami said. She made a toothy grin that very much reminded me of Yakishio. "Friends help friends, and they call each other out too. Whatever happens, Lemon-chan's gonna need us."

***

Asagumo-san finally got back to us some time later. She'd spotted them, and we were to regroup at the south side square.

Stands and vendors bordered the wide, open space. There seemed to be some kind of local farmer's market going on.

"Nukumizu-kun, you gotta try this. Even the bones are good."

Yanami had somehow already gotten her hands on some salt-grilled sweetfish.

I did my best to ignore the crunching and scanned the crowd for Asagumo-san. It didn't take long to find a short girl creeping around the back of the vendors. I opened my mouth to call out to her but quickly closed it again.

She was wearing a light orange one-piece dress and a classy wide-brimmed hat—the sort fancy actresses sometimes wore. Plastered on her forehead was a cold patch. Beneath that she had on a pair of mirrored sunglasses. Each element inconspicuous enough on its own, but together the ensemble looked positively insane. It made associating with her in public exceptionally difficult.

Yanami bit off the sweetfish's head. "So you know that girl, huh?"

"So do you now."

What a girl to lose to. Yakishio had it rough.

Finally noticing us, Asagumo-san pattered over.

"Um...hello," I said, not knowing how else to react.

Asagumo-san made a coy smirk and unpeeled the cold patch. "Didn't recognize me in this disguise, did you? It's me. Asagumo."

Wow, no way, I'm Nukumizu.

She reapplied the patch, implying *that* was the disguise.

"Is Lemon-chan here?" Yanami asked from a safe distance.

"They're on the opposite side of the plaza," Asagumo-san answered. "It seems they're touring the vendors in order. We can safely wait for them here."

She scurried off to hide in the shade of one of them. We went after her. She then pulled out that phone-like device with the antenna, removed her sunglasses, and studied the meters on it.

"Hey, how did you figure out they'd be here, anyway?" I asked. That thing wasn't a people-radar, was it?

"I collated and analyzed a statistically significant amount of data." She puffed out her tiny chest proudly. "And it just so happens my calculations were correct."

Yanami cocked her head. "How do you calculate something like that?"

"Devices help, but they come with a certain margin of error that I merely minimized through sheer volume and analysis," Asagumo-san expounded. "Through trial-and-error, I've managed to understand and account for the tracker's inaccuracies."

I didn't like the sound of that. "Did you say 'tracker'?"

"I'm using a GPS, yes."

Lord help us.

Yanami took another few paces back. "Is that, um, legal?"

"Quiet," Asagumo-san hissed. "They're here."

Yanami and I exchanged looks, then peeked out from behind the vendor.

The plaza was positively packed. From our vantage point, we had a good view straight down the middle, with the vendors lining either side.

"On the right. At the gelato place," she whispered.

I squinted until I could kind of make out a man and a woman among the crowd. The man was tall, handsome, and had glasses. The woman's tawny skin said enough. That was Ayano and Yakishio, all right.

Ayano wore a sophisticated, white button-up. Yakishio was in her uniform. We might as well have been staring into a soap opera.

They continued their rounds, gelato cones in hand. They smiled and laughed at each other in such an intimate way that any random person would have assumed they were on a date.

Yanami hummed. "Ayano-kun. Handsome guy. Tall too. Lemon-chan's not too bad herself. They look good together."

"Yanami-san!" I hissed.

Her hand zipped up to her mouth. "Sorry, Asagumo-san! It just slipped out."

"No offense taken," Asagumo-san said. "I agree with you. I always have." A self-derisive smirk snuck onto her lips. "Imagine my surprise when he actually agreed to go out with me. I thought I didn't have a chance." Her voice fell to barely a whisper. "I got lucky."

We didn't say anything. Couldn't. So we kept our eyes on our targets.

They stopped at one vendor after another, pointing, laughing, smiling. Yakishio shone like the sun.

I thought about what Yanami had said before.

You don't look at a guy who's taken like that. You just don't.

This couldn't have been easy for Asagumo-san. So I told her, "Hey, I think that's enough for today."

"They're moving on," she spoke over me.

I turned back to them. Yakishio was pulling Ayano by the arm over to another vendor that sold what looked like Western desserts. Self-serve, with baked goods out in the open for shoppers to grab and buy as they pleased. They were still working on their gelato. Ayano took a basket with his free hand. Yakishio tossed something in. They argued a bit—Ayano shook his head, grinning, and lifted the basket up out of reach. Yakishio jumped up and dunked in what she had anyway.

This went on for some time. Eventually, they blended back into the crowd, but Asagumo-san was still, her eyes fixed on nothing.

"Hey, are you okay?" I asked.

She pulled the cold patch off her forehead and spun around. "I'm fine," she said quietly. "Just gonna go touch up my makeup a little."

Yanami and I watched her head back into the station then let out a sigh.

"She's not doing so good," I said.

"No, she isn't. However sensitive you think girls are, Nukumizu-kun, double it."

Sugar and spice, I thought. *Maybe sugar and lipids in Yanami-san's case.*

Yanami put a hand on my shoulder and shook her head. "That comment earlier. About them looking good together? That was too much. Love is a complicated thing, and you need to be more careful."

"Are you actually trying to put that on *me* right now?"

"Sure am. Do something about it."

Why did I bother?

"Sure, whatever," I said. "Shouldn't you be going after her?"

"Me? Nah, dude, you go."

"She literally mentioned makeup. That means she's going to the bathroom. What am I gonna do, sneak in?"

"So you want me to chase her into the *toilet*?" Yanami argued. "Just wait for her outside. It'll be fine."

"Will it?"

"Look, times like this, what's important is just knowing someone cared enough to show up. Which, might I add,"—she frowned at me—"is the kind of support I wish *I* had from a certain someone." An incredibly fair point. Emotional labor was not my strong suit.

"Plus, I'm...not sure I really have any business talking to her right now."

True enough. The "they look good together" comment was a bit fresh.

"All right," I said. "I'm still not entirely convinced, but I'll go."

"Thanks."

I left the square and made for the nearest bathrooms for lack of a better idea, until I stumbled on an orange one-piece, hat-wearing girl stopped at a random store. She was eyeing a leather book jacket, hands behind her back.

"Asagumo-san," I called out. "Hey, are you, uh, okay?"

"Nukumizu-san," she replied without looking my way. She reached for the book jacket but pulled away at the last minute. "It's nice, isn't it? Do you think he'd like it?"

"I'd say so, yeah. Good eye."

"I thought so. Mitsuki-san does love his books," she muttered. "He wants to work with them in the future, you know."

"Really?"

I'd had no idea. Wasn't even clear to me what kind of book jobs were out there. Almost surreal how I was learning about a guy I barely knew from a girl I knew even less.

"He says being an author is more of a dream than a career plan. So he wants to go to Tokyo and study literature from an academic perspective. Maybe get into publishing. Anything, so long as it's to do with books," she went on to no one in particular. "I was surprised when he first told me. I'd never met anyone who shared my dream before."

"Right," was all I managed to say.

"Although personally, I'd like to be a librarian. Granted, it won't be any less competitive." She finally picked up the book jacket and felt the leather. "My calculations were correct."

"Huh?"

"I saw them," she said. "With my own eyes."

"Oh. Right."

I didn't consider GPS tracking a "calculation," per se.

"He doesn't like sweet things. I suppose it's possible he was getting them for me."

I nodded at mach speed. "Yup. Yeah, that's very possible. He's a nice guy."

"Yes, he is. He'll stomach gelato if you ask. Talk with you if you ask. He'll enjoy himself and smile like it too." Asagumo-san rambled like she was arguing with herself. She replaced the book jacket. "Has he ever...?"

The rest of her words were swallowed by the low drone of the station.

"We never got gelato," she said, louder. I stammered a bit, unsure how to respond. "We've never gone out to get dessert together. I never asked, because I knew he didn't like them." She grabbed the brim of her hat and pulled it down. "So it just...stung a little. Seeing them do it."

"Well, maybe he got a flavor that's not sweet," I suggested. "They do savory crêpes and stuff sometimes, right?"

"Savory? What kind could he have possibly been eating?"

"Maybe it was tuna mayo."

Asagumo-san's eyes went wide. "You think that whole cone was tuna and mayonnaise?!"

"Hey, it's a popular onigiri flavor."

I was totally BS'ing, but she laughed anyway. "That's one way to give yourself an upset stomach. I should look into light salads for him just in case." She looked down. "I'm jealous of Yakishio-san. She's so honest and unapologetic about herself and what she wants. I'm always so preoccupied with not being a burden."

"Eh, be a burden."

She looked back up in shock. "Won't he stop liking me?"

"Couldn't tell you. I don't know him that well. But he's probably not so shallow that he'd kick you to the curb for wanting to get ice cream."

I put up with a whole lot worse from a girl I wasn't even dating. That had to speak to something.

"You're actually very nice, Nukumizu-san," she said. "I had you all wrong."

Her and everyone else in school, apparently.

Asagumo-san peered up at me, studying me with those big, round eyes. "What?" I asked.

"Just wondering what the type of girl you'd fall for is like." She giggled. "I'd like to meet her one day."

"We'll see."

I liked girls well enough, but actually dating one, well—that was difficult to imagine right about now. Asagumo-san had herself a relationship and was up to her ears in problems. Yanami had none and still shouldered a completely different set of baggage.

It felt like the more people I met and the more I got roped into their circumstances, the less realistic genuine romance became.

"We should head back," I said. "Yanami-san's waiting."

"Of course. I'm composed again." She smiled. But not long enough to be relieved, because she jolted almost a second later. "Nukumizu-san! Hide!" She grabbed my hand.

"Huh? Why? What's happening?"

"There's no time! Hurry!"

With surprising strength, she yanked me all the way into a clothing store and into one of the changing rooms.

"What are we doing?!" I blurted.

"Hush! Mitsuki-san will hear you."

Had he snuck up on us? But then why were we hiding in the first place? I didn't see what was so wrong about us being "caught." Worst case, it looked like we were out shopping...alone. Together.

"Wait, crap, this might be bad," I whispered.

"Which is exactly why we hid!"

The rim of her hat jabbed me straight in the face.

"That kinda hurts."

"I'm sorry, but there's not exactly much room in here."

Changing rooms were not made for two. Asagumo-san shifted around to try and get the hat out of my face, her hair tickling my arm. Why did all cute girls smell good? I wasn't imagining it. They just did.

"He wasn't with Yakishio?" I whispered, ears perked.

"No. He was alone. I'm going to take a peek outside." She poked her head out of the curtain.

Now this was ironic. The Infidelity Investigation had itself become quite duplicitous. How the tables had been turned.

Asagumo-san brought her head back in. She grabbed another cold patch and pressed it on her forehead. "I don't know how to tell you this, Nukumizu-san."

"Give it a shot."

"I have been spotted."

"Pardon?"

She threw open the curtain. Waiting for us outside was an awkwardly stiff Ayano.

Asagumo-san bowed. "Hello, Mitsuki-san," she said, surrender in her tone.

"Chihaya," said Ayano. "And is that Nukumizu?! What are you two doing?"

What a question I wished I had an answer to. I didn't bother trying to offer one. Chances were I'd put my foot in my mouth, so I ceded the floor to Asagumo-san.

I shot her a glance. She returned it, then nodded. We were on the same page.

"Mitsuki-san," she began, taking a step toward Ayano. She turned, looked at me with her squirrel-like eyes, and suddenly I felt we were not on the same page anymore. "Nukumizu-san can explain everything."

***

Most people, when they hear "West Station," they assume it's an entirely separate train station. It is, however, just the way people refer to the west side of Toyohashi Station.

Ayano and I rode the escalator toward West Station together. We stepped off without a word, and continued walking without a word. Thanks to Asagumo-san's ridiculously bad idea of throwing me to the wolves, he and I had gone off to talk alone.

We arrived at the west entrance to the city's largest train station. The shinkansens stopped there, so the place was littered with shuttle services for people traveling from afar.

"Let's find somewhere quiet," Ayano said.

"Right," I agreed. "Privacy."

We glanced around. Ayano muttered, "This honestly might be our best bet actually."

"True. Not too many people."

Compared to the east side, West Station was fairly calm. We'd need that for what we were about to discuss. Honestly, it was almost *too* quiet.

Ayano stopped in front of a red Yamasa Chikuwa shop and turned to face me. There was no anger in his expression. Just a calm firmness.

"I'd like to know what I walked in on," he said.

"Right..." I put my hand to my chin and feigned thought.

On the inside, I was sweating bullets. What in the world could have possibly excused Asagumo-san and I being in the same changing room together? I had to remember I hadn't done anything wrong. I'd come here to help Asagumo-san, and this was the situation I'd been rewarded with.

Screw it, I decided.

I met his accusatory gaze with one of my own. "I think you're the one who has some explaining to do."

He frowned. "What? Why?"

"You're here with Yakishio, aren't you?"

The only reason I was on trial right now was because *this* guy was going around being stupid.

"She was helping me with some shopping," he said. "We weren't even together long."

"What about the city hall? Was that just a stroll you two were on? I can keep going."

I could not keep going.

Ayano said nothing for a while before throwing his hands up with a chuckle. "You caught me. Should've known I couldn't fool you."

"Y-yep. You totally should have."

Now here was a guy who didn't have the wrong idea about me.

"We weren't doing anything that we shouldn't have been, though," he added quickly, waving his hands. "You know Lemon's better than that."

He was right. However little time we'd actually spent together, I did know that.

But that was exactly why Yanami and I had gotten involved to begin with.

I shook my head. "Come on. Don't act stupid. You're going behind your girlfriend's back to hang out with another girl, and not just once or twice either. The girl being Yakishio doesn't excuse it. It makes it worse."

We both clamped our mouths shut when a customer emerged out of Yamasa Chikuwa. What a great spot he'd chosen for this.

Once the passerby had disappeared, I asked, "So what's going on with you two?"

Ayano flapped his mouth a few times, searching for an excuse, before giving up. "I was...asking her for relationship advice," he confessed.

That confused me. Asagumo-san was a little—scratch that, a lot—weird, but what problems could he have possibly needed an ear for? And from *Yakishio* of all people?

He looked away, scratching at his cheek nervously. "I've never dated anyone before, so I just don't know how any of that works, you know? I needed someone to point me in the right direction."

"And you picked Yakishio."

"She's popular. And she's got the female perspective and all that."

"I see. So you wanted relationship advice. From Yakishio," I parroted mechanically. What a fool. An absolute buffoon. Wow, my opinion of Ayano was at an all-time low. "What kind of advice exactly?"

"Well, uh, it's a little bit...private," Ayano said. "Don't repeat this, okay?"

"Can do."

Who did I even have to go blabbing to? No one. And how bad could it be? A guy like him asking a girl like Yakishio for help, it couldn't have been much more than a "How do I hold hands?"

"The thing is—Chihaya," he stammered, "she can be very... aggressive. When we're alone."

"Oh."

Little more intense than holding hands.

"I'm a guy, right? It doesn't bother me," he continued. "It's just, she never takes it any further than k-kissing. And I don't want to, well, cross boundaries too fast, you know?" He checked for listeners and lowered his voice. "I'm afraid of coming on too strong. I'm scared I'll move too fast or hurt her somehow. Or that I'll do something to make her hate me."

All of this was so unbelievably far beyond me. But things were finally starting to make sense. He hadn't been cheating on Asagumo-san. It was all just a bit of friendly relationship talk with... With who again?

"Wait, you told all that to *Yakishio*?!" I blurted. "You can't be serious."

"She's my only real close female friend, so, yeah."

"Wow."

How could I have forgotten I was talking with a neutron star? Even granting he somehow didn't pick up on her feelings, the balls on him to take those topics to a *girl*. My opinion of him was in an actual freefall. Pretty soon he'd get close to about where I placed Yanami.

"It's your turn," he said. He stepped toward me before I could process what the rules for the game were. "Give it to me straight. I can take it."

"Take what?"

"I know I'm not much of a man. I won't blame her for moving on, especially if it's with a guy like you."

I babbled and floundered. "Okay, hold on! Slooow down! You've got the wrong idea!"

Also, why did he have me on such a high pedestal? Like, seriously.

"Then why were you two together? You don't have to hide it."

"I'm not hiding anything! She was—"

I cut myself off. How much could I say? That Asagumo-san thought he was cheating on her with Yakishio so she stalked him? They were in a prime position to weather the flames of adversity and come out stronger for it, and I didn't want to be responsible for screwing that up. Things like that were bad for your conscience.

"She was what?" Ayano pressed.

"She was...helping me with my own relationship stuff!" I sputtered. "I was asking her for advice too!"

Ayano made a face like I'd just told him pigs could fly. That probably would have been more believable. "I didn't know you had a girlfriend," he said.

"I don't, but there's this girl, so, uh, I just wanted her take on stuff."

"The literature club is full of girls. Why would you..." Ayano got quiet, put his hand on his chin, and thought to himself. Presumably for real, not feigned.

"Hey, uh, you good?"

A distant speaker announced the arrival of a shinkansen. A few moments later, the bell chimed, sounding its departure.

Right on cue, Ayano clapped his hands. "I get it now!" I didn't. "Don't worry. I read you loud and clear."

"Uh, right. Yup. You got me." What in God's name had he got?

He relaxed for the first time since we started talking. "Everyone says I'm thicker than concrete, but I'm not blind."

"Hey, so, uh, what are we talking about?"

He patted me on the back. "The girl you like's in the lit club, isn't she? That's why you couldn't go to them."

I assumed he wasn't referring to any of the characters in the light novels on that bookshelf. In any case, I only had one option. I refused to be the cause of a breakup.

"Yeah, you caught me," I said.

"Lemme guess. Is it Lemon?"

I was ready for this and immediately shook my head. "Nah, not her. And don't worry about it. I'll manage on my own. You focus on treating Asagumo-san right."

That, of course, left Yanami and Komari as the remaining options. Two extremes but on the same spectrum.

"Hey, don't be shy. You should invite her out so we can all go hang out sometime."

"Er, uh, I'm good. It's sort of a secret? A big secret. Massive. Hoping to keep it under wraps until graduation at the earliest."

Ayano grinned. "I'm not saying you have to confess right away. Just take things a bit further, step outside the box. Establish yourself as someone more than just a clubmate." *Now* the guy had brains. Was selective emotional intelligence a thing? "I've got your back. I'll make sure Lemon's there."

"Yakishio? Why Yakishio?"

This man could have given the densest protagonist in the world a run for his money, and it was officially becoming my problem.

"Because you said she's not the one," he went on. "She'll just be there to help grease the gears and make the actual girl more comfortable going out. Heck, you could even get Lemon to ask her if you're too shy to do it yourself."

That might have been his first actually good idea all day.

"Wait, do *not* tell Yakishio I have a crush on anyone! *Especially* not in the lit club!"

"Oh, I know this trick. That's a good front you're putting up."

"That is not what this is! *Don't* tell her anything! At all! I'm being serious!" This was such a stupid thing to make my throat sore over.

"I getcha, I getcha. Don't worry. I'll take care of everything."

A thought occurred to me as I lamented the sheer lack of critical thinking being weaponized against me: Maybe he and Asagumo-san were the perfect couple after all.

***

"So you told him you were asking for relationship advice. About a girl you like. In the lit club."

Yanami's fit of laughter accosted my eardrum through the phone speaker. It was late, and I'd just gotten in bed.

"It's not funny," I grumbled. "I barely made it out of there."

"Fair enough. My bad." I heard her recompose herself. "But at least Asagumo-san knows the guy isn't cheating on her. It all worked out."

"I guess."

I'd relayed the gist of our conversation to Asagumo-san, skimming over the sensitive bits. She now knew Ayano's relationship with Yakishio was strictly professional. The rest was none of our business. Whatever discussion they needed to have, that was between them.

"So where we goin'?" Yanami asked.

"Where's who going?"

"Don't you have to ask out a girl in the lit club now?"

"Technically."

"Could be me."

"It could," I said. "You're cool with that?"

My luck might have been coming back around for once. Dealing with Ayano sooner rather than later was definitely preferable to leaving him to his wild imagination.

"Sure. Don't got anything else to do anyway," she said. "Just lemme know."

"Will do. Thanks."

Yanami's tone shifted. "Not like I have anyone else to hang out with. Everyone's too busy with their *boyfriends* to make any time for me these days."

I sensed danger. Had to end this call before we got any further down this dark path or we'd be at it all night.

"Yeah, so, that was pretty much it. It's getting kinda late, sooo..."

"You wanna know something, Nukumizu-kun?"

"What?" I asked like a dork.

"You are the actual worst at this."

In my defense, who *was* good at phone calls?

***

Futagawa Station was only a stop away from Toyohashi Station. A short walk from there was the Underground Resources Center. Despite its aggrandizing name, it was actually just a museum for (drumroll) resources obtained from underground. Pretty much every native Toyohashian could claim to have been at least once in their childhood.

There, two days after our stint with espionage, was where we had decided to meet.

What had I gotten myself into? That early afternoon, I was to play the leading role in Operation: Help Nukumizu With His Crush, starring Ayano, Asagumo-san, Yakishio, *and* Yanami.

Ayano was the only one pushing that angle, but that was enough to be a nuisance. Yakishio thought we were all just going out to have a bit of fun and little else. Yanami knew, of course, but her presence alone would clue Ayano in on who my supposed crush was.

I could already feel a headache coming on.

The plan was to survive the day first. Then I could tell Ayano she dumped me or something later and sweep this whole debacle under the rug.

"Wait, then he's gonna remember me as 'the guy Yanami shot down' for the rest of his life."

This incensed me for reasons unknown.

I didn't deserve this. The only reason I was in this mess was because Ayano couldn't keep it in his pants.

I checked my watch. The other four would be arriving by bus soon. Ayano, for all his defects, had instrumented this entire get-together with frustrating efficiency. The Resource Center idea was my only contribution. He had set up the group chat, collected schedules, and plotted out modes of transportation. The works.

"Nukumizu! Hey, hope we didn't keep you long."

Speak of the devil.

"Nah, you're right on time," I said. "Looks like we're all here."

"Yup." Ayano bumped my shoulder and winked. "You got this, bud." Urgh.

"Hello, Nukumizu-san. I've been looking forward to today." Asagumo-san's beam was just slightly eclipsed by the reflection from her forehead. Today she was dressed up in a striped blouse and tight, form-fitting pants. She really was cute when she wasn't triangulating your exact position.

"Hey, Nukkun," Yakishio chimed in. "Lookin' very Nukkun today."

She had on jeans and a white off-shoulder top. Simple yet fashionable and sophisticated. For once, she smelled like something other than deodorant.

Last in line was Yanami, wearing a greenish sweater with a translucent overshirt draped on top. A light brown skirt dangled just above a pair of thick-soled sandals. On her face was a mask of stone-cold apathy.

"You good, Yanami-san?" I asked.

"Yup. Just fine."

Whatever had made her grumpy, it was not my problem. Probably food-related.

I hadn't been to this museum since elementary school. The long, dark passage down into the earth evoked nostalgic memories.

Ayano pushed up his glasses, surely sharing the sentiment. "Ready to go, Nukumizu?"

"As I'll ever be."

No man could resist the siren call of the museum, be they scientific or historical. So we ventured forth. The path into the exhibit hall was cragged and moody, modeled after a mine shaft. When we reached the bottom, it was like the subterranean world had opened up for us.

Both Ayano and I gasped in awe. The former sped off toward the mineral samples.

I was considering where to begin my own journey, when Yanami yanked me by the collar. "A moment, please."

"What?" I griped. "I wanna get going."

"After we talk. This way."

What was her problem? Yanami dragged me all the way to the edge of the hall, pouting the whole way.

"What's the big deal?" I asked again.

Yanami planted a hand on her hip and answered me with a sour stare.

"We are five high schoolers. On summer vacation. Out. Together. Need I spell it out further?"

Yes, actually, kinda. What were those? Buzz words for her new ad campaign?

"These are the best years of our lives. And you want us spending them underground? Literally. We are *underground*," she ranted. "Where's the aesthetic, dude? Who picks a place like this?"

I didn't know many people other than me, so I wouldn't know.

"Ayano was cool with it," I said. "Guys love stuff like this."

"Great. Love that for you. But have you considered, oh I dunno, the other half of the population? Look at my fit! Look at how hard I went on this!"

"Right. Why did you, by the way?"

"What part of this are you not understanding?!" Yanami erupted. "This is what you *do* when you go out with people! Especially when there're other girls! Don't you wanna turn heads? Even a little?!" I didn't, really. No. "God, *that* is your problem, Nukumizu-kun. Right there. I'm sure this is like the coolest thing ever to boys, but to us?"

She pointed.

?
Sum

Asagumo-san was off in her own world across the hall. "Look! Everyone! Come see this incredible specimen of mica over here! Gosh, how many capacitors could this baby make?"

She and Ayano were glued to the display case, having the time of their lives.

I turned back to face Yanami. "Your point?"

"W-well she doesn't count! She's smart!" Yanami shot back. "Lemon-chan'll get me!"

The implication of that statement was not lost on me.

Over in another corner, the traitor cried, "Holy crap, guys! They've got a mine cart! Are we allowed to ride it?"

"Yakishio! Do not touch that!" I snapped at her.

The sophistication went only fabric deep with her.

"Her too?" Yanami slumped over. "Am I...alone?"

"Hey, it's not so bad. Look over there," I said. "You can touch a bunch of metals and compare weights and stuff. Wanna try that?"

She looked up at me, pitifully. "I guess that sounds...kinda interesting."

"Then c'mon. Strike while the iron is hot."

She groaned. "That wasn't funny."

We headed over to the exhibit, Yakishio soon catching up to us. "Hey, Nukkun, was this your idea?"

"Ayano approved it. Going out in general was all him, though."

"Oh yeah?" Yakishio had a mix of suspicion and curiosity on her face. "When'd you guys get so close?"

"We were just talking. Came up in conversation."

"Whatever you say. Mitsuki was just tellin' me some funny stuff before, is all. Like that I should have your back, whatever that means."

"My back, huh?"

Why? What had that astronomical anomaly done? I just wanted a quiet life. Was that too much to ask for?

This was all Asagumo-san's fault.

"What's going on, hm?" Yakishio pressed. "Lemme guess..." She glanced toward Yanami, who was struggling with a metal sample.

"Holy jeez, this is heavy!" She grunted. "You guys come help me!"

Look who was having fun all of a sudden.

Yakishio nudged me with her elbow, smirking. "I'm your wingwoman, eh?"

"No. Absolutely not," I said.

Nightmare. I was trapped in a misinformation nightmare. That was what this was.

I spun around, searching for Ayano to give him a piece of my mind. I found him and his girlfriend admiring a theoretical model of the city's future made back in the Showa era.

Yakishio followed my gaze. Something left her when she saw them.

"Wanna, uh, head over?" I suggested.

"What, and make their bike a four-wheeler?" She flashed her toothy grin. "I wanna leave 'em be for today."

"I mean—"

"What's the deal, man?" She did a little more than nudge me in the ribs that time. "I'm their cheerleader, Nukkun. The sidelines are where I belong."

"But he doesn't even know how you feel. Can't you at least—"

"No," she interjected again. Softly but nonetheless surely. "It's fine."

She smiled at them, and I saw peace in it. I realized then that she *had* come to terms with her feelings. She loved Ayano. She would continue to love him. But if it meant being at his side, she was willing to forever keep it under wraps. As easy as it would have been to distance herself or just vent those feelings to be done with them, Yakishio chose persistence.

I hadn't given her enough credit. Not for the weight of what she carried. Not for the pain. And certainly not for her strength.

"I owe you an apology, Yakishio."

"Why?"

"You're always smiling and goofing about something," I said, "so I forget sometimes that you've actually got a decent head on your shoulders."

"Very perceptive of you." She made another eyes-shut, toothy grin and held a couple of fingers up in a peace sign. "If you're really, really sorry, you can show me your summer homework."

"Uhhh, which subject?"

"Whaddya mean 'which subject'?"

She was a goner.

Yakishio read my blank expression. "I'm still keeping up with the picture journal, for the record! It's technically part observation diary now, though, 'cause I have these morning glories I've been logging."

"That's not gonna be in the homework."

"Crap."

I took it all back. All of it. Sophisticated? No way. This was the headless horsewoman.

"Sure, whatever, we can meet at the club room and I'll—"

"Excuse me," Yanami butted in, "why do I smell something sappy going on over here? And screw you, sharing homework without me."

Surprise, surprise, Yanami hadn't done jack either.

"Yana-chan, you still have homework too? We gotta have a copy party," Yakishio said.

"For sure. At Nukumizu-kun's place."

I wished I had a say in this conversation.

"I'll give you my stuff so take it somewhere else," I said. "Whoa, would you look at that? It's a quiz game. You guys should totally see who's smarter. Bye now."

Free at last, I surveyed the hall. Those loess doll samples were calling my name. They were fascinating, really. A sort of mass of minerals that formed in the soil around—

"Nukkun! There's room for three players!" Yakishio waved me down.

I, of course, already knew that and had skillfully neglected to mention it. To no avail. I continued to pretend not to hear her until Yanami joined the chorus of shouting, and my hand was forced.

Me versus Yanami versus Yakishio. A fierce battle it would not be.

***

We exhausted the exhibits in about two hours, so we moved things along to the Audio-Visual Education Center next door. The fact that we had the option of two museums in such close proximity may have informed my choice of location for today.

A couple of overstimulated kids darted in front of Yanami in her chair. She struck a pose.

"Got it." I returned her phone.

"Thanks. Good photo. Think it'll pop off? I'm worried the crystals are kinda overpowering the vibe."

Yanami's throne was a concave chair coated in a zillion little colored "power crystals" all on the inside. It certainly made for a striking backdrop.

"Nah, the people love you," I answered robotically.

I stretched. Yakishio was off studying Japan's Largest Acorn from every angle. Ayano and Asagumo-san were taking turns snapping pictures of themselves in front of a trick mirror that made you look pencil thin.

My batteries were dry. Home called.

Yanami flipped through a pamphlet and *ooh*'d at one of the pages. "They got a planetarium," she murmured. "A planetarium..." She chewed on that for a while. I made a conscious effort to ignore her mad musings. She sneered. "So *that's* your angle. Oh, boys. They will be boys."

I could come up with a few things wrong with that statement.

"There's no angle," I said. "What are you even talking about?"

"Hey, no, I get it. Believe me. We're not so different, you and I." Somehow I doubted that. She got up and plopped her hand on my shoulder a couple of times. "We're high schoolers. It's summer vacation. We all want our five seconds of fame, deep down. What's your social media?"

I did technically have a Twitter, but none of my zero followers would be turning any heads no matter what envy-inducing snapshots I decided to post.

"Not my thing, and I was actually thinking about going home pretty soon."

"Wait, what? No, but the rocks were to get my guard down so you could come in clutch with the planetarium. That was the plan, right? Right?!"

Clutch? Not unless she was talking about cars. In which case, still no.

"We can check it out if you want."

"I knew it! I'mma go get the others!"

While Yanami ran off to collect the three stragglers, I was left to ponder extroverts and the nature of their existence. And by the time I'd gotten bored spacing out at an exhibit, Ayano had gotten us tickets. Leave it to the guy with the girlfriend. He worked fast.

Yanami quietly stared at her ticket.

"What? You're the one who wanted to go," I jabbed.

"Sure, but like, did you see today's program?"

I hadn't. I checked my ticket—"Protect our universe with the Super Galactic Spectro Rangers!"

"Sentai. Nice," I said.

"Is it?" said Yanami. "I'm not sure sentai's gonna be romantic enough for what you're going for. You think it'll work?"

For whatever she had in mind, probably not.

Yakishio leaned in. "Oooh, Spectro Rangers. I used to love them."

"You've seen this one before?" I asked.

"My dad once bought me this science-y picture book from here. He said to read it lots so I'd get real smart."

And it had worked like a charm.

By some miracle, I managed to herd Yanami toward the planetarium with us. Only once her attention was occupied with selfies did I feel confident enough to take my eyes off her for a second.

Asagumo-san had her eye on a poster. "Mitsuki-san, it says there's a mystery to solve as part of the show. What do you say to a little contest?"

"I like the way you think," Ayano said. "How about you join us, Lemon?"

"Huh?" Yakishio stopped taking pictures for Yanami for a second. "Me?"

Ayano sidled up to me and whispered, "It's all you. You got this."

"What? No. Can we not?"

He nodded in understanding he did not even remotely have. "You're nervous, but don't be. We'll still be there. Just a few seats away." I didn't get a chance to rebut. He waved Yakishio over. "C'mon, Lemon. It'll just be the three of us."

"Uh, but I was gonna watch with Yana-chan," Yakishio said. "You and Asagumo-san go ahead."

Perfect smile. Perfect play. She'd done well. Now the bride and groom just had to take a hint.

"You don't have to be considerate," betrayed the bride. "I've been wanting us to become better friends."

Yakishio wavered a bit before shaking her head. "Thanks, really, but you seriously oughta keep Mitsuki some company. Let's go, Yana-chan. Nukkun." She spun around.

Ayano grabbed her by the hand. "Lemon, wait! Listen—"

A moment of hesitation. "Mitsuki!" she growled, shaking him off. "You're here with Asagumo-san, so you watch with her! I'll watch with them! Now stop! No buts!"

Several guests stole glances our way, wondering about the commotion.

Finally getting a clue, Ayano lowered his head out of the almost literal clouds. "I'm sorry. I didn't mean to upset you."

Asagumo-san came and put a gentle hand on him.

"Look," said Yakishio, awkwardly scratching her head, "she's your girlfriend. I dunno why you're prioritizing anyone but her."

"You're right."

"I know I am. Sheesh, man, that wishy-washy junk's not what made me fall for you." She smacked him on the back. "I can tell you that much."

I caught her grin. Everything she said, I echoed. No guy that had earned Yakishio's attention had any business being that...

"Wait," I interjected, her words finally registering. "Yakishio, what'd you just say?"

"What'd I what?"

She was still grinning. She repeated the question, gaze moving first from Yanami to Asagumo-san. Saw the looks on our faces. And then, all of a sudden, hers went from tawny to sheet white.

But she still had a chance. The only person who didn't know already was Ayano himself, and he was denser than something dense.

If ever there was a time to be dumb as a brick, it was now.

I slowly, ever so slowly, turned to gauge his reaction. Of all the times to grow a brain.

Ayano was redder than a tomato. "Lemon, did you just...?"

"N-now listen first, Mitsuki! I-I can explain! It's not— I didn't mean—" Yakishio avoided his gaze, hiding behind her hands. She slowly backed away. "I didn't mean to... I didn't..."

She kept repeating combinations of those words, each utterance quieter than the last. And then there was nothing. Yakishio whirled around and flew like a bat out of hell, weaving and dodging between people.

She was gone in an instant. Those of us left were still grappling with what we'd just witnessed.

"I...guess she's gone," I said.

Time unfroze. As it did, Ayano started to run—but barely made it a step.

"Don't go!" Asagumo-san shrieked. He stopped. She clasped her hands together like she was begging. "Please, don't go! You don't have to! You can stay here! With me!"

"Chihaya, she's—"

"*I'm* right here! Me! Your girlfriend!"

She *was* begging now. Pleading. Tears welling in her eyes.

Ayano approached her after one last glance in Yakishio's direction. Just one. Before the first tear could fall, he caught it in a handkerchief. "You're right. I'm sorry," he said.

"Mitsuki-san..."

Watching them hold each other, I felt something. So vivid, I couldn't bring myself to give chase.

"Nukumizu-kun!" Yanami shook me. "Hey, Lemon-chan's still out there!"

"I get it."

"What?"

It hit me all at once. It was grief. Some part of me, some little sliver, didn't want this ending. Some part of me wished he had gone to her. It was a selfish part of me—a stupid part of me that thought that Asagumo-san's misfortune and Yakishio's resolve were obstacles to the true happy ending.

"I'm going after her!" I blurted.

I ran. I left it all behind me and didn't look back. People flitted by. At some point, I think I practically jumped down a flight of stairs. Still, she was nowhere to be found.

I exploded out of the building.

This wasn't like me. And it most definitely wasn't the business of a background character.

But right now, Yakishio didn't have a protagonist to make it theirs.

***

I came to a bus stop a ways down the street, lungs on fire. Yakishio was there, crouched down on the concrete. Behind the guard rail at her back was a big supermarket parking lot. The scenery never much cared for context.

A dull pain burned in my chest as I stepped up next to her. "You all right?"

"Nukkun?" Yakishio lifted her head up from her knees. Her eyes were red. "I know I'm stupid, but I sure blew it fast, didn't I?" She hid her face and wiped the stains off her cheeks.

"They're managing back at the museum. Everything's good there."

"Thanks. And sorry."

"I'm...sorry too," I said.

"What for?" She smiled. I wasn't buying it.

I looked away. I felt guilty because half of me had hoped I wouldn't find her. Because I knew I wasn't the one she wanted to see.

He would never come. She could wait as long as she wanted, forever even, and he still wouldn't. And the moment I showed up, that truth would sink in. I would be the cold breeze that snuffed out that hope for good.

Cars rolled past the small, two-lane road in front of us. It was never quiet for too long. Life never cared much for circumstances.

Yakishio pulled herself up and stretched, hands against her hips. "I'm okay now. Just gonna wait for the bus and head home."

"I'll go with you."

She shook her head. "Let a girl have some time to think by herself."

"Then at least let me stick around until it gets here."

"All right, sure. Then chat with me."

"Chat? About what?" Ah, I had heard of this technique. A simple request was never what it seemed when spoken by a pretty face. The internet said so. "Um, uh, have you decided what you're doing for the club journal?"

Yakishio was not pleased. "That was your cue to make me laugh and feel better." See? Never what it seemed. "Oh, well. It works. I was thinking of writing a poem or something."

"You know how to write poetry?"

"I'm not *that* dumb. You start it with 'once upon a time, yada yada,' stuff happens, you take it from there."

"That's a fairy tale, Yakishio."

Yakishio gave an offhanded, "Whatever you wanna call it," and then she cleared her throat.

"Once upon a time, there was a girl," she began. She saw my mouth hanging open, and a shadow of a smile briefly appeared on her lips. "She loved, loved, loved to run. And then, one day, she met a boy. The boy loved, loved, loved to read."

It took me too long to realize this was about them. Yakishio and Ayano. I held my breath, nearly forgetting to breathe.

"The boy liked to talk about his books, and the girl liked to listen. They became best friends," she continued. "But what the girl didn't know was that the boy was a prince. And when the prince grew up, he'd have to go away to his castle. The girl wished she could go with him, but she didn't know the right manners or how to dance at balls."

A truck rumbled past, kicking up dirt. When it was quiet again, Yakishio picked right back up where she'd left off. "That made the girl sad, so the prince tried to teach her those things—how to have manners and dance at balls. The girl did her best to learn so she could go to the castle with him, and then, one day, she did. And they lived happily ever after."

I said nothing. Waited. No continuation came, though.

"What happened to them after they went to the castle?" I asked.

"They lived happily ever after. Like how all stories end."

The bus pulled up, its brakes creaking and hissing. There was a puff of air and the door opened.

Yakishio hopped up onto the first step. "This is me. Tell the others I'm sorry for all that."

"That's it?" I called out. "This is how it ends?"

She stopped climbing the steps but didn't turn around. "How what ends?"

"You and Ayano."

"Yes." Her voice barely cut over the purr of the engine. "It is."

For a beat, it seemed like she was going to say something else. She didn't. The door shut behind her as she climbed the last step.

I stood there until the bus was long out of sight.

***

I flipped my workbook shut. Wasn't making any progress on tonight's homework.

Three days had passed since then. About to be four, according to the clock. Yakishio wasn't replying. Yanami had spoken with her friends, and they said she wasn't going to track practice either. Ayano and Asagumo-san had called me at least a half dozen times between them, asking for updates. I told them the truth, that she seemed in surprisingly good spirits, but not the whole truth. I never could find the right words to explain what we talked about at the bus stop.

Four days remained of summer vacation. Surely, she would show up again when the semester started.

If I could let it go for that long.

My phone lit up. "Asagumo-san?"

I read the message and jumped straight out of my desk chair. I darted to my window. A tiny silhouette was pacing outside our house.

Throwing on whatever clothes I could find and hurrying as quietly as I could, I stepped outside. There, loitering beyond our front gate, was Asagumo-san.

She flung her head down as I slowly came up to meet her. "I'm so sorry for bothering you so late," she said. The hour of the night was probably only part of the reason for her frail voice.

"Don't worry about it. What are you doing here?"

As if I didn't know already. She was cognitive dissonance walking. She hadn't done a single thing wrong that day. She was well within her rights to speak up and stop Ayano when she did.

According to Ayano, though, that didn't stop her from beating herself up. It was pretty bad, apparently.

"Have you gotten in touch with her yet?" she asked.

I shook my head. "Still getting left on read. Which I guess is better than nothing." Empty consolation.

Asagumo-san hung her head. "It's my fault for being indecisive," she rasped.

"How? Why?"

"I said I was prepared to stand aside. But when it came down to it, I got scared. I should never have said anything."

I didn't know what to tell her. "Dating's hard, I'm sure. That's why you, y'know, work together. Work through things. Uh, trigger events. Get all those...CGs. And stuff. I guess."

I offered a silent apology. I was too pure a boy for matters of love.

"If only it were that simple." She shook her head. "All I've felt since dating was anxiety. Worry. I can't stop thinking about all the what-ifs."

"Lemme ask you this, then. Why did you let it play out? Why didn't you ever step in and stop them from meeting? Wouldn't that have nipped this whole—"

That wasn't right. She didn't need to be talked down to. She didn't need me to tell her things she'd surely told herself a hundred times already.

"I'm just so terrified of saying the wrong thing," she said. "Like I did when he tried to go after her."

"That wasn't the wrong thing. Yakishio's the one who screwed up. Ayano shouldn't have gotten his priorities twisted either."

"I'm not so sure. He tried to go. I had to stop him. I manipulated him."

"You're his girlfriend. You had every right to call him out."

"And they had every right to speak, but I robbed that from him. Because I was afraid that if they did, I'd lose him. That he'd pick her instead of me. It wasn't courage or bravery that made me speak my mind. It was because I doubted him." She sighed languidly. "I'm so tired. If Yakishio's the one he prefers, I'd rather just end things now than—"

"That's not the answer," I said firmly.

"But I—"

"It's not. I may be talking out of my ass right now, and call me out if I am, but you didn't ask Ayano out on some whim, did you?"

"No."

This wasn't my business. I was an outsider. There was a time to stop and it was before I'd even said anything. Problem was the bed had been made.

Time to lie in it.

"Well, from what little I know of Ayano, he's not the kind of guy to say yes on a whim either." I thought of the last time I saw Yakishio, moments before that bus door closed. "Now take all those emotions and stuff them in a box. Yakishio feels the exact same way, only she's trying to know her place." Asagumo-san jumped at her name. "She doesn't want to come between you two. So please, none of those drastic measures. She's my clubmate. When push comes to shove, I'll have her back."

Asagumo-san looked confused. "Then wouldn't you *want* us to break up? For her?"

"Nothing would hurt her more than being the reason you two couldn't stay together. Please. Don't treat her like a victim. You think you're helping, but you're not."

"I..." She hung her head again. "I'm sorry."

I saw her start to shake. Then I realized I may have said too much.

"Wha—hey, Asagumo-san? You're not crying, are you?" A girl sobbing in front of your house after midnight wasn't a good look. I whipped around to Kaju's room on the second floor. No lights on. Was I crazy, or did the curtain just move? "Look, um, hey, I didn't mean to come down so hard on you. Here." I patted my pockets. No convenient tissues or handkerchiefs. Thanks, God. "Okay, uh, I'll walk you home part way at least. Are you close?"

She nodded. I walked with her down to the main road.

"You don't have to worry about her," I said. "I've got it."

In a much more real sense, I kind of didn't. I had no grand plan. Seeing Asagumo-san like this, though, I had to give her something to cling to.

She reached into her pocket and pulled out a device. "At least let me give you this. It may help. I've already adjusted the GPS parameters."

"I'll...manage without. You should too, for the record. Promise me you'll quit it with those."

She nodded, and we parted ways. I had a lot to think about on my way back home.

Nothing came to me. I mostly found myself wishing magic were real. I could snap my fingers and solve everything. How was I going to interact with her when she did inevitably show her face again?

My phone buzzed in my pocket. The caller gave me pause—lit club vice president, Tsukinoki Koto.

"Hey there!" her voice came over the speaker. "Didn't think this'd actually go through this late."

"Yeah, I'm up. Bit weird that you are, but what's going on?"

"So do you remember me saying Shintarou trashed my first draft for the journal?"

"Vaguely."

"Well," she said, "that got me feeling spiteful, so I edited it to be all-ages for real this time. Could you give it a once-over for me?"

Why was she not studying for college exams?

"Can't Prez do that?" I pointed out.

"He'll just trash it again. I want *you* to do the editing phase so we can say it technically had one, then sneak it in all guerilla style."

She was out of her mind if she thought my word held that much sway in that club.

"So you're looking for a scapegoat is what you're saying." Silence. It spoke volumes. "I'm sorta busy lately, but send it over and I'll skim it, I guess."

I started to hang up.

"Wait," I heard her say. "This part's important." I put the phone back to my ear, wishing she had led with this. "Yanami-chan told me about what happened with Yakishio-chan. Sounds like a lot."

If it had come from Yanami, there was really only one thing it could have been.

"How much?" I asked.

"All of it. From the cheating arc to the foot-in-mouth in front of the girlfriend. Pretty much every detail."

I sighed. "She loves to talk, doesn't she?"

"Don't hold it against her. The track team captain asked me about her, so I'm the one who picked Yanami-chan's brain."

Yakishio was their ace. I supposed it was only a matter of time before they started getting worried. The question then became what Senpai wanted me to do about it.

"You free tomorrow?" she asked. "Well, today technically."

"Uh, before I answer that, you've got to clarify why you're asking."

Tsukinoki-senpai did. Loud, proud, and without a hint of irony. "For the intervention, obviously!"

Too Many Losing Heroines!

LOSS 3

Let He Who Is Without Loss Cast the First Stone

THE SUN SOARED HIGH THAT LATE MORNING. I cracked open a can of coffee and glanced sideways at the sign above me. "Roadside Station—Mokkulu Shinshiro." We were almost an hour north of Toyohashi by car.

"What am I doing here?" I mumbled.

I hadn't had much of a choice. The moment I saw that minivan with the rookie driver sticker on it and Tsukinoki-senpai popping her head out of the driver's seat, I knew. This was my life now. Komari and Yanami were already inside too, so there was *really* no way out. Still, had I known I would be whisked away all the way to the neighboring city with nothing but the clothes on my back, I might have put up a bit more of a fight.

Shinshiro was a city situated at the rocky mouth of Oku Mikawa, the northeastern tip of what was once the Mikawa Province where the Battle of Nagashino was fought, like, forever ago. I didn't know much else about the area. Point being: We were in the middle of nowhere with mostly mountains for company.

If Tsukinoki-senpai was to be believed, and Yakishio was staying with her grandmother in the city, then we still had a long journey ahead of us. Hence the quick rest stop. Though "quick" was just wishful thinking.

I sipped on my coffee, waiting and wondering when Senpai would get us back on the road. "Oh, right. She sent me her draft."

She'd give me crap if I didn't get that over with. I found the message and clicked the file.

Literature Club Summer Activity Report: Tsukinoki Koto—The Writing Beauties in the Wood

Sunlight trickled through overhead branches. The man walked wearily, his kimono a burden with its flowing fabric.

"How much further, shrimp?"

Before the man flitted and flew what appeared to be a minuscule person about the size of a mere starling. Insect-like wings protruded from the creature's back.

The little creature answered without words, sweeping upward in a dramatic arc. The man strained his eyes. Not far up the path was a quaint yet cozy-looking building of an almost European aspect.

"How extravagant." The man tossed the creature a coin, pleased with his own snide comment.

His guide vanished along with the coin into thin air.

Dazai was at first apathetic when Mishima had initially informed him of Kawabata's presence in their new world. Upon hearing the old author had been appointed shepherd for their fellow reborn, however, apathy became obsession. Two days by carriage it had taken him to reach the ivy-strangled, two-story little hovel in which Kawabata toiled away most of his days. Dazai thought it unbecoming of their station.

No maid took notice of his arrival, however long he waited, so he tried the bell. Dazai knew his lines and exactly what he would say—preparation rendered useless when *he* was the one who answered.

"Ah," Kawabata spoke first. He cast a cold gaze upon Dazai. "Come in. I'll put on some tea."

Inside was barren of the comforts of their previous world. Unsettlingly small for how large the exterior appeared, the room could only be eight tatamis at most. For furniture, there was little more than a table and chairs that Dazai now sat at.

Kawabata's attire, though originating locally, had the quality of a Christian priest. He prepared tea in front of a small stove, his back to Dazai.

"Have you no maids?" the latter commented.

"I find their services redundant in these parts," Kawabata replied. "Nothing a little fae help can't manage."

Dazai considered the room. One corner pronounced itself among the rest. There were flasks and beakers and a workstation not unlike what a chemist might have.

"Ever heard of nilkeene grasses?"

"I haven't," Dazai said to his host's back. "Good for dementia, I hope."

Kawabata poured steaming water into a teapot without so much as a chuckle. "Through careful extraction, I've found they can be made into a most handy solution. Odorless and tasteless, but the tiniest bit before bed and you'll never have a sleepless night again."

"A sedative."

"Really, you'll be out like a light." Kawabata set the table with cups, still disregarding Dazai's comments. "One could do whatever they liked to you in the meantime. And you'd be none the wiser."

"You dabble in questionable fields. Pardon the irony, but I'm beginning to doubt the safety of drinking such a thing."

"Ah, but is insomnia itself not a plague we writers are far too familiar with? It's even more potent than Calmotin, you know." Tea cascaded beautifully into one cup. The golden liquid proffered steam which rose and clutched at the air enticingly. "These leaves were gathered in the Solidea Highlands. Comparable to Ceylon in taste."

Kawabata slid the near-brimming cup over to Dazai. Dazai did not immediately reach for it.

Just then, the door swung open. Three young girls flew in, chattering and giggling like little birds.

"Teacher, won't you play with us?"

"Look! It's a stranger!"

"Who is that?"

Each girl's hair was some otherworldly shade of green or blue. These children were certainly not human.

"Now, now," said Kawabata. "I have a guest. Off you go."

The girls made their displeasure known, though departed nonetheless as noisily as they had come in.

Dazai regarded the door with fatigue as it slammed shut. "And who were they? They didn't look like any elf I've ever seen."

"Shrewd eye," Kawabata mused.

"Graceless things. A single waitress carries more refinement than the three of them together."

"And yet they all sleep with closed eyes." Kawabata directed his squarely at Dazai. "But where were we? Ah, yes. Tea. Please, drink while it's hot."

"Of course." Dazai reached for the cup. "But first," he stopped, "a question for you. You know where Akutagawa-sensei is. Tell me. Please."

Kawabata stared. Dazai lost the silent battle and averted his gaze.

"I found myself in the possession of some sort of 'skill' when I first arrived in this strange place," Kawabata digressed. The steam became less enticing, less defined. "'Words of Power,' it was called. Any who assents to what I say, regardless of what that is—regardless of what is in that tea—must ultimately carry out that which they agreed to do."

Only then did Dazai notice his hand moving on its own. "Kawabata-san. What is this?"

"I said to drink. You said 'of course.' My words have power, my friend."

It wasn't just his hand. Dazai's entire body defied him. Every muscle acted to one singular goal: drink the tea.

And he did. The steaming liquid filled his mouth, poured down his throat, and seeped into his stomach. Even as it scalded his flesh the whole way down, Dazai could not stop.

He hurled the empty cup onto the ground. The drug was exceptionally fast-acting.

"Perhaps I should have let it cool more," Kawabata cooed. "Though it really is best when it goes down hot."

"What is the meaning of this? What are you going to do to me?"

"You will not see Akutagawa-kun. Not you. Not anyone." He drank his own tea. Cold, calculating eyes pointed themselves at one side of the room. "You're too stubborn for your own good, so I'm simply going to dissuade you *physically*."

Gritting his teeth against the searing pain in his esophagus, Dazai followed Kawabata's gaze. Among the aged walls, scars of time worn like badges of honor, was one less ancient. As if it and its accompanying door had been built just recently.

At last, Dazai placed the unease he had felt upon entering this place.

The room *was* too small for its exterior. The rest, Dazai surmised, laid beyond that new wall.

"The nilkeene should be taking effect any second now."

"You drank some yourself. I saw you," Dazai rumbled.

"A house secret. We wouldn't want to waste perfectly good tea now, would we?"

Sarcastic conceit smeared itself across Dazai's expression. "And here I was almost worried about you."

"Why is that, Dazai-kun?"

"You see, I switched our cups while you were distracted with those girls. And you didn't even notice."

Kawabata flung the liquid from his cup, eyes widened in shock.

Dazai scoffed. "Believed me, did you? Cute." He stumbled to his feet, the lethargy passing.

"What's happening? Did you swap our cups or not?" Kawabata demanded.

"My skill is 'Liar,' Sensei. Anyone who believes my lies makes them true." Dazai found the vitriol emanating off of Kawabata's person almost endearing. "I never switched the cups. You never swallowed any nilkeene, but you did swallow my deceit."

The villain fell to his knees. Dazai knelt down, tearing the string from the breast of Kawabata's shirt.

"I suppose you'll have your revenge now, won't you?" the disheveled man snarled.

"I've long given up the past, old dog. What we have in bad blood there is good in equal measure."

Dazai hoisted up the feeble-framed man and carried him to the out-of-place door. Inside was a simple room. At its center, shadowed in the dim light, a single large bed. Something sweet lingered in the air.

"We've plenty of time to make up for both. Now you *will* tell me where Akutagawa-sensei is, or we're going to find out together how you sing."

***

I didn't want to meet the families that considered that family friendly.

After I was done watching clouds pass in a cloudless sky—and contemplating modern day censorship rules—I wandered into the rest stop. Yanami was standing at the nearby snack corner with her arms crossed all serious.

"What're you up to?" I called out to her.

"Hey. Perfect timing." She had her eyes fixed on some goheimochi.

Goheimochi was a rest station staple here in central Japan—rice mushed together into mochi, molded into an oblong rectangle, skewered, drenched in a miso sauce, and then grilled right on the stick.

"Hungry?"

Yanami replied, "I had a thought about carbs."

"Just one, huh?"

"Just one. So, like, ten thousand years ago, humans stopped being hunter-gatherers, right? They started farming. That is to say, they switched to a life of carbs."

"Deep. There more to that?"

She nodded like this was world-shattering business. "Ever since, it's been a staple of our diet. Our histories have been intertwined, one synonymous with the other. Think about it. Are we truly the masters? Or are we merely living in the carbohydrate's world?"

"Just say you want the goheimochi."

She shook her head. "It's not about the mochi. It's about reevaluating relationships. Carb-related relationships."

I didn't follow, but I kinda didn't need to, honestly.

"This is totally about how you ate all that somen and—"

"*Didn't* gain weight," Yanami snapped. "I've been hot every day of every year since I was born."

"Not to rain on your parade, but I saw on TV the other day that scientists are saying our daily carb consumption probably didn't actually go up all that much after switching to farming."

"Wait, no kidding?"

"I mean, it's in the name. They hunted *and* gathered. We didn't go chasing deer for every meal. We ate nuts and plants and stuff like that."

Yanami crossed her arms again. "What you're telling me is I should go for the goheimochi."

What I was telling her was she wasn't fooling anyone. I went for my wallet.

"Hold it," she said. "Are you seriously about to eat that in front of me when I'm *specifically* trying to not think about it?"

"Sounds like a you problem. I haven't had one of these in forever."

"What if..." She squinted at me out of the corner of her eye. "Just one bite?"

"Too mushy to share. We'd make a mess."

"Are you implying I'm a mess?"

"A hot one, hopefully. I hear hypothermia's bad for you."

And just like that, I wasn't hungry anymore.

I left Yanami to her starchy considerations. We'd been here long enough, so I went looking for Tsukinoki-senpai. We were supposed to be on our way to talk to Yakishio.

I found her and Komari chattering over at the gift shop.

"I still think ume jam belongs on the left." Senpai clunked the jar on the shelf.

"N-no way. Right." Komari clunked it on the other side of a box of venison curry.

Tsukinoki-senpai held her fist up to her mouth and frowned. "I just can't see it. Curry's got the *oomf* factor, I'll give you that, but left still doesn't click for me. I don't buy that the jam has the 'troubled upbringing' vibes I need from the right."

"Th-that's why it's perfect there. New wave."

What in God's name had I walked in on?

Tsukinoki-senpai noticed me before I could make up my mind about getting involved. "Allow me to explain, Nukumizu-kun."

"Please don't."

"Listen anyway. You see, the common fujoshi has long been discriminated against, and it's only gotten more and more out of hand. There are those who claim we would ship a pencil and an eraser given the opportunity." She put her face in her hand in a dramatic gesture of indignation. "The audacity. Can you believe such slander?"

"Is that not what I was just witnessing?"

"What you were just witnessing was a thought experiment." A degenerate one, by my approximation. "What you need to understand is that, when a new anime comes out, being on top of the shipping is a matter of life or death to us. We need to constantly be in peak condition, our synapses ready to fire. Consider the way athletes need to work out. That is what this is to us proud members of the literature club."

I didn't feel safe in this club anymore.

"I read you loud and clear. Wish I didn't but here we are," I said. "So what was all that left-right stuff about?"

"In standard notation, the name of the top goes first, the bottom second," Senpai elucidated. "Top goes on the left, bottom goes on the right."

Komari nodded fervently. "Th-this lets us debate in public."

Just because you could didn't mean you should.

"So the jam's the bottom, er, sorry. On the right," I said.

"Wrong. Incorrect. The jam is the top."

"I-it's the bottom!"

Tsukinoki-senpai squinted and thought again. "So the curry's the top? Spicy's too on the nose. It's too one-note."

So much for the code.

"Y-you don't get it," Komari argued. "H-he hurts with his touch..."

Senpai clapped. "Oh my god, you're so right! Forbidden love. The harder they yearn, the harder they hurt. It's brilliant! It's so workable!" She bit down on her lip and the spark faded. "*Gah*, but I've already set my heart on the jam!"

"It happens." Komari nodded sympathetically.

"Hey, uh, Senpai?" I chimed in. "Can we leave yet?" The fujos set their sights on me. "Wh-what?"

"Fine." Senpai flicked her chin at me. "You make the decision."

"D-don't screw it up." Komari glared at me through her bangs.

What had I done?

"Uh, all right. How's this?" The two bore down on me while I threw together something random on the shelf.

"Adding the pork ramen... That's inspired," Senpai breathed.

"He's a n-natural."

Oh. Oops. That wasn't the curry. My mistake.

"All right, now that that's settled, let's get out of—"

Senpai snatched me up. "Come with me!" She dragged me to another shelf. "Let's go again with these pickles."

"Y-yamagobo..." Komari muttered.

"Impressive first pick, Komari-chan."

The small one giggled.

They went off all over again, this time over...pickles. We weren't going anywhere anytime soon.

***

A blur of green flitted by my window. We'd been on the road going on four hours now, and that was just after leaving the rest station.

"Where even are we?" I muttered under my breath.

Tsukinoki-senpai was anything but focused. The longer we drove, the more detours she decided to make, and the further from Yakishio we got. I had to say something or we'd be stuck out here for the rest of our lives.

"Senpai, can we please go to Yakishio's place now?"

The car jerked. Senpai pumped the breaks and cut the wheel far to one end.

"Right, turn signal first," she mumbled.

"S-Senpai, those are the wipers," Komari stammered, and not entirely on account of shyness this time.

"Ah. Wrong lever."

"P-please watch where you're going."

Nothing like a driver fresh out of school. This was nothing new, of course. Yanami and I had had a perfect view of the show the whole trip from the back seats. Komari did a good job at keeping it entertaining for so long.

Tsukinoki-senpai peered back through the rearview mirror. "Were you saying something, Nukumizu-kun?"

"I was asking if we're even headed to Yakishio right now."

"I've got it this time. I know where we're at. Have a little faith in your senpai." She cackled.

I'd heard that exact promise back at the Nagashino Castle Ruins. And then again at the hot springs we'd killed way too much time at. Somewhere along that course of events, my faith left me. We were straight up sightseeing now, and it wasn't even a secret.

Honestly? Wasn't as bad as I made it sound.

"I will, for lack of a better option," I said. "Though the lack of civilization has me somewhat concerned."

"Yeah, been wondering about that. Anyway, on an unrelated note, Nagano's just down that way if we keep on this road. Neat, huh?"

"Hardly unrelated, if you ask me. I'd prefer to stay in Aichi, please."

The car jerked again. Yanami blinked her eyes open. "Bwuh? I was sleepin'. We there yet?"

"Not yet," I said. "You're drooling."

"Am not." She took my tissue and wiped her mouth anyway.

Forget the drooly one, I scolded myself. *Tan one first.*

I leaned forward. "The sun's gonna go down soon. Are we close or not?"

"Relax, we're close. Super close," Senpai insisted. "Whew, Grandma Yakishio sure is *a ways out.*"

I checked the map on my phone. "We're twenty minutes away from the rest stop. I thought you said we had a ways to go from there."

"Look, if I told you the place was a hop away from the rest stop, you would've been on my butt about going there ASAP." Indeed I would have. It was, in fact, the whole reason we were out here. "Sometimes you gotta take your time in life. I wanted to cruise a bit, okay?"

"I'll call you free-spirited, because that sounds nicer, but we're not out here to cruise. We're here to—"

"You're doing it again," Yanami cut in. "See the way you always jump to negative, negative, negative? That right there's what I'm talking about. We got to go to a hot spring, see some cool stuff, and eat some good food. Isn't that enough for you? 'Cause it should be."

I noted the grain of rice clinging to the self-righteous grin on her face. As far as she was concerned, she'd gotten a good soak and some katsudon out of our day trip. The nap must have been killer too.

"But we drove out here to see Yakishio," I said.

"...Yeah. Duh."

She had absolutely forgotten.

Wait, why was I the only one surprised about this information?

"Hold on a minute. Yanami-san. Komari," I accused. "Did you two know we were gonna do all this? Am I the only one who didn't get a damn itinerary?!"

The accomplices sniggered.

"No fighting, kids," Senpai cajoled. "Get mad at me if you must get mad at someone, Nukumizu-kun. Just know that I was eating it up the whole time. You make pushing your buttons way too easy." She smirked at me through the mirror.

I hated that she knew exactly how to weasel her way around a situation like this. The best way to get someone to shut up was to kick the nest until they realized you were doing it for the fun of their reaction.

"We're fine, promise. This time for real," she said. "I've got her address up right now."

"Fine, whatever. How'd you get it anyway? She's not replying to anyone right now."

"Track team captain, remember? I sorta looked after her during my time in the student council, so we keep in touch. We talked to Yakishio-chan's mom together."

She used to be in the student council? She'd met Yakishio's mom? That sentence was too packed.

"Now I have even more questions, but putting those aside," I said, "basically, her mom wanted us to go check on her. That right?"

"Right. Her and her grandma know something's up. They're as worried about her as the rest of us." She glanced at the navigation. "Just about there. Get your tears and speeches ready for the reunion. No teasing the criers."

The navigation did its whole "you have now arrived" spiel as Tsukinoki-senpai pulled the car into a wide shoulder.

"This is it," she said. "Anyone got eyes on the place?"

I didn't see much but trees and thick shrubbery all around us. "You sure about that?"

Yanami opened the window and stuck her head out. "There's a sign over there for tire chains?"

Yakishio was many things but surely not a forest dweller. The three of us looked to our chaperone.

"U-uh, this is the address I was given." Tsukinoki-senpai fiddled with the navigation, flustering under the pressure. "I-it should be here."

"Should we call her mom?" I suggested.

"I didn't actually get her number. My track friend should have it." She gave her a call. No answer. She left a message, then flumped back in her seat. "Guess we wait now. Anywhere anyone wanna go in the meantime?"

Yanami's hand shot up. "Yeah, there's a totally aesthetic spot near here! Can we go there?"

"Sure. Where's it at?"

Yanami studied the map on her phone. "Uhhh, a bit north of here. Follow the road, then take the side road past the sign on the left."

"We're on our way!"

Wheels screeched against the pavement, the acceleration flinging us back into our seats. Komari squealed.

With Yanami's directions, we were there in just three minutes.

Tsukinoki-senpai slowed and pulled us onto the shoulder. "This looks like the place." Off to the side, a narrow byway descended toward a nearby river. It would be a tight fit for the car. "No parking lot, looks like. I'll just stay here. You guys check it out."

"You sure?" I asked.

"I'm waiting on that phone call anyway. Gotta call Shintarou too, while I'm at it."

"Prez?"

"I, uh, maybe sorta kinda skipped a study session for this today. Need to cook up a few excuses."

She would need full concentration for that. Her boyfriend kept a short leash.

The rest of us followed the path down to a riverbed. The river itself ran perpendicular to the byway, fast but otherwise relatively shallow, and looked about ten meters across max. At its narrowest point, a small, concrete bridge connected our side to the opposite. In fact, it was so small it didn't even have any safety railings. Calling it a bridge might have been overselling it.

Yanami shoved her phone toward me. "That's it! That's the bridge! I'm gonna stand up top, you get me from down there and try not to drown. It's gonna do *numbers*!"

"You'd be out a phone, if that changes your opinion at all."

"Nah, it's insured."

I was too, technically.

Yanami scurried up onto the bridge, beamed, and flashed double peace signs. "Get the picture!"

Thankfully, I could get a decent angle from the riverbed and was spared a watery demise. If I positioned the camera so her feet were just out of frame, it sorta looked like she was standing in the river. Not a bad shot, actually.

"Hey, Komari, you might as well get up there too." I glanced around for her. She was peering into a crevice between two rocks. "What're you doing?"

"I s-saw a crab."

Now I was interested.

I crouched down beside her. "Where? In here?"

"D-don't talk so much. Y-you'll scare it."

Wise. I shut up and strained my eyes. Something shuffled deep inside. The hunt was on.

I heard a *clack*. Weren't crabs supposed to go *snip*? I strained my ears this time and heard the noise by my feet. I turned around.

Yanami wound up her arm, and half a second later, a large rock hurtled straight toward me from the bridge.

"Whoa!" I yelped. "Hey, you can't throw rocks at people!"

"How long am I supposed to keep posing for, dude?! I look like an idiot over here!"

Full transparency: I had completely forgotten about her. This loser was justified in casting her stones.

"Okay, that was my bad," I admitted. "I got caught up with this crab."

"You were in the middle of my photoshoot. And you ditched me. For a crab. That better be the most amazing crab in the whole friggin' world."

That was what I was trying to find out. The pinchers were pretty cool, she had to admit.

For the sake of avoiding being stoned, I appeased the Yanami and took her picture.

"Did you get it? How do I look?" she said. "Better than the crab?"

"Way better. The crab is so jealous."

"Sound less interested, why don't you. Hey, Komari-chan, you wanna take one with me?"

Komari croaked at the sudden attention. "I-I'm...looking at the crab."

"Again with the crab." Yanami sighed. "What is with this crab? You wanna eat it or something?"

People did feel things other than hunger, contrary to Yanami's belief.

"Hey, cheer up," I said. "Why don't we take a video or something?"

"A video! Great idea. Good to have you back, Nukumizu-kun."

When did I leave? *What* did I leave? Those mysteries frightened me.

I let the camera roll while I zoned out and took in the area. Yakishio's grandma had to be close. I wondered what kind of person a Yakishio two generations back could be like.

It occurred to me that Yanami was not moving.

"Gonna be a boring video," I told her.

She started fussing with her hair. "Okay, but I don't actually know what I'm supposed to do. I figured I could sing, but I don't know any lyrics."

"Nursery rhymes are songs. Do 'Little Elephant.'"

"That just feels sad. You sure?"

I was not.

Yanami ended up just waving her hands around. Boring may have been putting it lightly.

In the middle of filming, a figure wandered into frame. A figure with short hair, long limbs, and tawny skin. I almost couldn't believe it. Almost shouted even, had she not winked and held a finger up to her lips, signaling me to keep quiet.

Yakishio slinked up behind Yanami, who had caught sight of my hanging jaw. She cocked her head at me. "What now? Is it a king crab this time? A snow crab?"

Yakishio got right behind Yanami and held her arms out wide.

"Little more rare than that," I said.

"Wait, for real?! Is it a horsehair?" Yanami swung down and forward to scour for the nonexistent crustacean just as Yakishio threw her arms around her.

Momentum happened.

"Uh-oh," was all I could mutter.

Yanami pulled Yakishio down, and Yakishio pushed Yanami right over with her—straight into the river. There were screams.

I decided it wasn't my fault. It was gravity's. There was even video evidence proving that it was expressly not my fault.

I stopped recording and went to help. Had this been a judo match, how legal would that move have been, I wondered.

***

I let the cabriole sofa take me and the high vaulted ceiling fill my entire field of vision.

Thanks to the directions of a dripping wet Yakishio, we had made it to her grandmother's house. It was the furthest one back in a small little community. Western-style, surprisingly enough for an older occupant, and two stories. Apparently, it had been put on sale as a vacation home before Yakishio's family renovated it for themselves.

Her grandma lived there alone, on account of her husband working abroad. Currently, though, she was out shopping.

Past the overlook on the second floor, I could make out numerous rooms along the hallway. The one we sat in was furnished modestly, though the fancy English books cramming the tops of shelves betrayed a living that was anything but.

Yanami and Yakishio were in the bath. Komari was being devoured by the couch. Tsukinoki-senpai, meanwhile, showed little inclination of removing herself from a massage chair.

I went over to her. "Hey, can we talk?"

"About what, young one?" she warbled. "As you can see, I'm tending to my aches and wounds. Ahhh, that's the spot. I can feel my bones popping back into place as we speak." At least one of us was in heaven.

I glanced at the bathroom. No sign of Yanami or Yakishio. "I'm real happy for your bones, but what's the plan now?"

"Plan? What plan? Our beloved Yakishio-chan is in good spirits. That's all that matters." Senpai returned to her warbly moaning.

"That's what worries me. If she was obviously down in the dumps, we'd have a leg to stand on, but how do we even broach the subject if she's not even acknowledging it?"

Yakishio hadn't cracked once since her comedy sketch of an entrance. I knew her well enough to figure that was her way of coping with something.

"You're about as quick to jump to resolutions as you are conclusions," Senpai said. "Slow down a bit."

"I... Okay."

"Pretending to be okay is *part* of being okay sometimes. Relax. Just be there for her." The massage chair puffed, then stopped vibrating. Tsukinoki-senpai hopped up and shook a dozing Komari. "All yours, Komari-chan."

She jumped. "Huh?! B-but I don't...need a massage."

"Sometimes you don't know whatcha need till you try it. Thisaway."

Senpai hauled her over, and Komari got plunked into the chair with another of her surprisingly feminine yipes. If only she were that cute normally.

"Oh, I see you've found my best friend." Yakishio appeared, working her hair with a towel. The tank top and shorts look was made for her. "I use that puppy pretty much every day."

"Didn't get hurt or anything, did you?" I asked her.

"I'm fine, worrywart. Didn't expect to go head over heels that easily, though. Yana-chan's surprisingly heav—"

"Surprisingly *what*?!" Yanami barked from the changing room. "You say something, Lemon-chan?!"

"No! I didn't finish it!"

"But you started, you little...! Oh, forget it. Just get over here! And be subtle about it!"

"I forget something?"

Typically, subtlety didn't involve shouting across the entire house. Yakishio went over, did whatever it was she needed to do, and then jogged back to grab Yanami's bag.

"She okay?" I said. "Did *she* get hurt?"

Yakishio waved me off. "Nah, nah, she was just having trouble fitting into some of my—"

"I said *subtle*, Lemon-chan!"

"Sorry! Forgot! I only said it to Nukkun, though."

"Okay, fair enough."

Lovely knowing where I stood on the matter.

I was beginning to think I might have imagined all that drama four days ago. No one was addressing it. Relationships proceeded as normal. I only wished I could join them.

I surrendered to the couch. Yakishio soon joined me. I smelled soap and a bit of citrus.

"So what were you guys doing there?" she asked.

"Just hanging out," I lied. "Wasn't expecting you to pop up, though. That's for sure."

"'Pop up'? What, like I'm some kinda cryptid?" We laughed a little. Paused. "You talked to my mom, didn't you?"

"Huh? I..."

"Thanks. For caring, I mean." She stood before I got the chance to read her face.

The front door clicked open and an older woman stepped inside. "I'm back, Lemon. Do we have guests?"

Aside from the streaks of gray in her hair, you'd never tell from her posture that she was over the hill. The wrinkles on her face seemed deliberately made to accentuate her features rather than betray age. No doubt, she'd been gorgeous in her youth. It didn't take a master detective to tell who she was.

"Hey, Grandma!" The younger Yakishio hurried over to help with the bags. "Some friends from school were in the neighborhood, and we kinda got soaked, so I went ahead and let them in."

"Playing in the river again, were you? You better not have dunked anyone."

"Nah, that part was on accident."

Her grandma was about to say something when Tsukinoki-senpai showed up. "So sorry for barging in. We're in the literature club with Lemon-san."

"Welcome, welcome," said the grandma. "Glad to have you. I hope no one got hurt on account of my granddaughter."

Senpai accepted her hand and shook it. "No. The other one's just borrowing your bathroom. We really do appreciate Lemon-san letting us in."

"Well, good. It's a relief to hear she didn't drag you by the hair."

She shot her granddaughter a look. Yakishio shrugged and stuck her tongue out.

"Lemon-chaaan, where's the ice cream? You said there'd be ice cream." Yanami emerged from the bathroom, towel around her neck and cheeks flushed pink. The second she recognized who had joined us, she stood to attention. "H-hello! Thank you for having us! I'm Lemon-san's classmate, uh—"

"Welcome," her grandma greeted. "I apologize for my granddaughter's antics. Lemon, have you served them tea yet?"

"On it! Also, I'm gonna take some ice cream." The Yakishios disappeared into the kitchen.

Who could have guessed that Yakishio two generations back was shockingly normal.

Yanami came and sat next to me. She and Yakishio must have used the same shampoo and stuff, but somehow, she smelled different. This scent was sweeter. "So Lemon-chan told me in the bath that her grandma used to be a college professor."

In other words, Yakishio came from a family of intellect.

I reflected on this. "How?"

"I dunno, man."

The Yakishios returned with a tray full of tea and ice cream.

"Make yourselves at home," said her grandma. "And please, stay for dinner too." Were we staying that long? She clapped. "You know what? We should have sushi. Anything anyone can't have?"

"Oh, it's fine, we can—*mgh!*" Mid-sentence, a cushion found its way directly in my face.

"I'll have it all, ma'am!" Yanami cheered, pressing even harder.

"Y-Yanami-san!" I grunted. "Can't...breathe!"

"Hey, how about shut up."

I could now accurately claim to have been smothered by a girl. There was definitely an angle I could take with that to make it sound impressive.

***

Night fell more quickly in the mountains. Mostly on account of the mountains, since there were hills for the sun to hide behind.

I sat at the table, staring up at the darkening sky through the skylight in the ceiling. The moon was out, but the stars weren't any dimmer for it.

"You better eat before it's all gone," Yanami said, shattering my reverie. She inhaled an eel nigiri, put a hand to her cheek, and did a wiggle. "It melts in your mouth! Can I steal the ginger?"

She yoinked the whole pile without waiting for an answer and immediately downed half of it at once.

"What happened to your carb arc?" I said. "That's a lot of rice you're eating."

"I'm just snacking less. Beauty is balance, Nukumizu-kun. Carbs *and* fats have their role in the process, and you can't... Do you not eat your sushi whole?"

I pretended not to care and finished the other half of my tamago nigiri. Who was she, the sushi police? "It gets tiring chewing all that at once. I like to take my time, thank you."

Yanami looked genuinely perplexed. "You can get...tired? From eating?"

Exasperated, I placed a platter of inari and maki in front of her. "Look at these rolls. See how huge they are? Try and eat one of those in one bite. I dare you."

"Oooh, can I?" She did exactly that. Into thin air, one of the extra thick maki rolls vanished. I wasn't even salty. Just impressed. She swallowed in record time too.

"You know what? Maybe it's a skill issue."

"I dunno what that means, but good luck with that. Oh, can I have another hamachi?"

There went another hamachi. I began to notice a negative correlation between the fullness of the platters and proximity to Yanami.

"You better get eating too, Komari," I said. "The sushi's flying."

She was presently doing silent battle with a roll of ikura. "I-I've...never actually had caviar. I'm k-kinda scared to try it."

Firsts were important. I left her to it.

I checked on the others while I slurped some red miso soup. Tsukinoki-senpai had actually hit it off pretty well with Yakishio's grandmother. They were locked in a lengthy conversation about cooking, though I chose to ignore the occasional reference to "wife training" from Senpai. She wasn't *actually* betting on setting up shop in Prez's kitchen...was she?

Yakishio loaded up Komari's plate with the fanciest pieces she could find. "Eat up, Komari-chan."

"U-uni? And is that a m-mushroom?"

"It's abalone. It's good. Real tender."

"I've n-never had either of these before."

Ah, summer. The season of firsts for many young men and women.

After a healthy six pieces of sushi and one inarizushi, I called it. I took a peek at Yakishio while I let it all settle with some chawanmushi custard. We never did talk about the obvious, and we certainly couldn't in front of her grandma.

Yakishio set down her bowl of red miso, noticing me staring. "Something on my face or what, Nukkun?"

"Oh, um, just wondering when you plan on coming back."

"Dunno for sure. Leaning toward staying until the day before school starts at least." She lidded the bowl, grinning. "Which I'm not ditching, just so you know."

Better than nothing, I supposed. I finished off my chawanmushi and thanked her grandmother for the food.

Yakishio seemed fine. She ate fine. Thank god she wasn't in Ayano's or Asagumo-san's class. Maybe it was safe to hope for things to drift themselves back to normal. There didn't need to be an "ending," or any kind of resolution necessarily. Life wasn't clean-cut and pretty like a video game or a novel.

Sometimes we just had to live without knowing what the "something" was. Without closure.

To borrow Yanami's words, maybe showing up—maybe caring—really was enough sometimes. It would have to be for now at least.

***

The sky was dark, and the platter I'd set before Yanami now lay empty. Komari was currently in the middle of a life changing moment after trying uni for the first time. Tsukinoki-senpai's conversation with Grandma Yakishio was just as energized as before.

"Don't you ever get lonely living so far out here?" the former asked the latter.

"You're never really alone when you've got the internet these days. And my granddaughter lends me her company every now and again." She reached over and patted Yakishio on the head, who grinned bashfully.

I waited for a lull in the conversation and said to Tsukinoki-senpai, "It's getting pretty late. Are you going to be good to drive?"

"I got us here, I can get us out. Sheesh, you never stop worrying." She simpered as she brought some tea to her lips.

She couldn't blame me for that after this afternoon's trauma. Not that I had much choice. I sipped my tea with grave finality.

"Hey!" Yakishio blurted. "You guys should just spend the night! We've got plenty of room!"

No one said anything then, so I obliged. "The offer's nice, but no one packed anything."

But then it hit me. I ventured into the past, into the annals of my memory, excavated past images. Yanami had changed into new clothes after the river incident. Everyone else had bags.

Everyone except for me.

I looked at Tsukinoki-senpai. "We're staying the night, aren't we?"

"It was always a possibility. That's why I said to pack." She blinked, her brain processing. "Wait, did I forget to mention that to you?"

As a matter of fact, she had. Why, God? Why was she like this?

"I brought literally nothing," I said. "And we can't impose anyway. That'd be rude."

No one could just host four people out of the blue. Grandma Yakishio must have been feeling pretty awkward.

"That's a fantastic idea!" she cheered decidedly un-awkwardly. "We'd love to have you!"

Come to think of it, Yakishio's mom had known we'd be coming. It wasn't a stretch to assume her grandma had as well and prepared accordingly.

I slowly raised my hand. "I, um, didn't bring any overnight stuff."

"You just leave that to Granny!" She gave what I assumed was meant to be a reassuring thumbs-up.

Yakishio did the same. As did Yanami. Followed by Tsukinoki-senpai.

Komari dithered a bit before she caught on and ultimately fell victim to the same disease.

You know what they say. If you can't beat 'em, join 'em.

***

Yakishio's grandmother led me to one of the rooms upstairs where shelves stretched all the way to the ceiling. Their contents consisted mostly of engineering books, and many were even in Japanese this time.

"Excuse the mess," she said. "My husband's overseas so he won't mind you roughing it in here for the night." She handed me a neatly folded pair of pajamas and some fresh underwear. "I'll get you a toothbrush too. Is there anything else you need?"

"N-no. That's okay. Thank you."

Here was a unique kind of uncomfortable. The kind you only got from exceptionally kind strangers.

As if she could read my thoughts, she lowered her head. "I'm sorry if all this is a little sudden."

"Huh? Oh, no, it's okay. You don't need to apologize."

"You all came for Lemon, is that right?"

"I... Yeah," I confessed. "That's the long and short of it, ma'am."

"I wish I knew what was eating at her, but I understand that some things you just can't share with family. So I'm glad she has you four." She gave me a gentle look, like she might a small child. "You're not *quite* how I pictured you would be, but I'm rooting for you. Granny's got your back, Nukumizu-kun."

"Thank you?" I was flattered? "So she's told you some stuff, then."

"Oh, I've heard all about you for a while now. I didn't think we'd get to meet just yet, though."

For a "while now"? That didn't add up.

"Wait, I should clarify I'm not her boyfriend or anything, and we've only known each other for a few months," I said.

"Oh. Really?"

I nodded. "I think you're confusing me for someone else. But I have a feeling I know who." I chose my next words very carefully. "He...may or may not be the reason she came up here to begin with."

Yakishio's grandma chose hers with the same care. "And this boy also isn't her boyfriend?" I shook my head. The silence said things I couldn't. "I understand. And thank you. All the more so."

"I mean, to be fair, we aren't, er, entirely unrelated. To what happened."

Personally, I had half a mind to debate that, but the other half knew it would be a losing argument.

"Well, should I take it back then?" My mouth hung open in confusion. She urged me with her eyes, but to what end? "I know I'm biased, but I really do think she's an attractive young woman."

"Huh. Well, yeah," I agreed. "She's popular at school."

Granny winked in a way that made her look frighteningly similar to Yakishio herself. "Better move fast then."

"I'm sorry? I don't follow."

She opened the door, a subtle smile on her lips. "Like I said. Make yourself at home."

***

Dinner ended with Yanami the undisputed champion thereof. Everyone was wiped, and no one wasted time getting ready for bed once the table was clean. The last to drag herself off was Yanami, who'd collapsed on the couch in a food coma for a hot minute. Calm came to the living room at last.

"Didn't know she could even *get* full."

It reminded me of the kind of gap moe you'd see when a typically strong and willful character showed weakness. If you could describe a food coma as "moe." I'd have to consult the experts on that one.

I fell into bed, too tired to even begin to take stock of all the things buzzing inside my head. Thankfully, sleep came almost immediately.

An unknown amount of time later, I stirred awake. I blinked at the clock and squinted in the darkness to discern that it was at least past midnight. The metaphorical cotton in my mouth motivated me to get up and head downstairs for something to drink. I was extremely glad in that moment to have gotten prior permission to pilfer anything from the fridge.

I nabbed some mineral water and was about to head back upstairs when I noticed someone sitting in the dark living room. "Yanami-san?"

"Oh, hey." Bubbly as ever, even in the dead of night. I took it the sushi had settled. "Still up?"

After a bit of waffling over whether I should or not, I took a seat across from her on the couch. "Got thirsty. Yakishio asleep yet?" The girls were all bunked up in the same room.

"Said she was gonna go for a run."

"This late?" I started to get up before quickly thinking better of it. I didn't know this area. Bad idea, unless I wanted to get lost. I cracked open the cap on my water.

"Yeah, I got a bit antsy too." Yanami threw her arms up and stretched.

I listened for anyone else who might have been up and listening, then said, "You guys talk at all?"

"About the elephant?" I nodded. She shook her head.

"Figured. It's tricky to bring up, huh?"

"I guess that's part of it. But also I feel like if we did, I'd say something I would regret." I waited for her to explain. "The whole reason I stepped in was because I wanted Lemon-chan to have someone on her side in all this. I just, how do I put it...?" She stared up at the ceiling, considering. "I dunno. I just feel like everyone screwed up here."

"How so?"

Yanami frowned. "Asagumo-san's feelings are valid, don't get me wrong. I get being insecure, especially in a new relationship, and with the way Ayano and Lemon-chan looked together—all that stuff. You see him do things and show sides of himself you've never known about, and it's like..." She fidgeted and picked at her fingers. "But also, that's just how it is. That's their relationship. They have the history, the shared memories, and she knew that going in. If it was making her uncomfortable, she should've talked to him, plain and simple. Instead, she played games and put them on trial, and I just don't think that's fair."

Yanami took a moment to breathe.

She shut her eyes. "Speaking personally, I'd bet money Karen-chan went through the same thing. She probably couldn't help but see me when she looked at Sousuke sometimes."

I thought about that. "Yanami-san, were you stalking—"

"I meant figuratively!" She sighed. "You never learn, I swear. Anyway, what I mean is like, she has to deal with Auntie treating her differently, or how he's already used to girly things most guys wouldn't be. It's not hard to put two and two together and realize that I'm the reason for all that. And like, all it takes is one thing out of place in his room to get your mind racing, and he's definitely got more than *one*. There's so much stuff I got him or things we bought together."

Assuming, that is, he hadn't thoroughly liquidated all such items.

Yanami scrunched her face. "Unless they're already past that stage," she said to no one but herself. "Are they? I mean, how wouldn't they be? God, it's too late for this."

Thus began the spiral. I had to end it now.

"Hey, you want me to get you some sugar cubes or something?" No answer. Yanami was too busy gibbering prime numbers to herself. "Uh, should I be concerned?"

She slapped her knees. "New record! I'm good." A beacon of hope in this dark hour. "Where was I? Oh yeah. So Karen-chan doesn't put Sousuke on trial, and she puts a...well, *tries* to put a healthy distance between us, but to be fair those one times were her trying to be nice. Point is, she'd never pull what Asagumo-san was doing."

"At least part of that's on the boyfriend, though," I interjected.

I didn't really have a point to make. Something about the way she was going off just made me feel weird. I couldn't really explain it any more than that.

"Sure, I guess." Yanami pouted, her train of thought derailed.

"Ayano's not a bad guy. I'm not saying he is. I'm just saying being dense isn't an excuse for doing stupid things. You can't blame Asagumo-san for feeling like her back was against a wall."

"But she—"

I held my hand up. "Let's stop talking about this."

Yanami scowled. "What's up with you?"

"I dunno, I just don't like hearing you be so hard on someone I guess. I dunno." What was I even saying? I was about to start cringing at myself. "Sorry. That was weird. What I mean is you can leave the hating to me."

"Gotcha!" She shot up to her feet. "One last thing, though. Lemon-chan sucks at being subtle! This was a dumb way for it to come out and she shoulda said it a year ago!" She was one to talk. Which she continued to do. So much for one last thing. "If Asagumo-san and Ayano-kun really love each other, they should've communicated more! This is the stupidest thing ever and those three need to get their shit together!" She let out a breath like steam from a machine. "All right, I'm done. Back to sweet, lovable Yanami-chan."

"W-welcome back."

Phrasing aside, she had a point. Ayano and Asagumo-san didn't talk as much as they should have. Yakishio may have done some leaping before looking, but the starry-eyed couple had let it happen.

"Still, though, I'm Lemon-chan's friend. If we talk, I know what I'm gonna say," said sweet, lovable Yanami.

"What's that?"

Yanami put on a face I had no words for. An expression I never thought she could make. "I'd tell her to go for it." I couldn't look away. Even in the dark, it blinded me. "I'd tell her if Asagumo-san's willing to just lay down and give up, she has no reason not to take what she wants."

"But you know—"

"She would never do that. I know. And, as lame as it is, it's the right thing to do." She sank back into the couch, back to her bubbly self.

I drank some water to fill the lull.

Moments like these kept me from forgetting we were worlds apart. Yanami had lost, yes, but she'd also loved. She knew people and she wasn't afraid to speak her mind or be herself around them. Sometimes, to be completely and fully honest, I couldn't help feeling small around her. Childish. Immature.

"I'm gonna go for a walk," I said.

"This late?"

"Moon's pretty tonight. Won't be gone long."

Things were coming to me in a way I wish they had when it mattered. I thought about Yakishio, how sad she looked getting on that bus, and how, in that moment, I'd froze up.

Yanami looked at me blankly, then softly said, "There's a shrine we passed on our way here. It's close by."

"What about it?"

"I hear that's where Lemon-chan goes when she wants to think." Yanami rubbed her eyes groggily.

I sulked. "Didn't say I was going looking for her."

"No? Then I'll go." That smug smirk I hated crept across her lips. "And I'll turn her into a hater too."

"Can we please not?" One was more than enough.

Resigned, I hoisted myself up.

***

Gravel crunched beneath my feet. I tugged at one of the sleeves of my shirt. I'd changed back into the clothes I'd come in. They needed a wash, but pajamas didn't lend themselves well to serious conversations.

"Sure hope she's there."

The roads lacked street lights, so when I stepped into the shadow of one of a million trees, where the moonlight couldn't reach, I could hardly even see my feet.

Eventually, they hit pavement. I opened the map on my phone, distressingly aware of my remaining battery. The shrine was just up ahead.

I stepped off the road, toward it, and everything opened up. Towering cypresses shaded the shrine's grounds. A cloud passed in front of the moon, casting everything into deeper darkness. I stood stock-still.

Something struck the ground. I whipped toward the noise. Nothing.

I waited. Still nothing. The cloud drifted away, and moonlight filtered through the cypresses again, revealing a lone figure.

Something struck the ground again. Yakishio bolted, her feet scraping against the dirt.

She stopped almost at once. Combed her hair back with her hands. Sweat trickled off her and twinkled in the moonlight.

The word "beautiful" came to mind and stayed there.

Yakishio returned to her starting position and bolted once more, again stopping after only a few strides. She did that several more times, and I kept watching. By the time she finally saw me, I'd lost count.

It was a surreal few moments. Like I was looking into a painting, and it was looking back.

"Oh. Nukkun," she said, nonchalantly brushing her hair back again. "Fancy meeting you here."

"Heard you went out for a run and couldn't help myself."

"I could use your help, actually. Been practicing my start. Time me." She tossed me a stopwatch. I juggled it a few times before grasping it. "Start when I start, stop when I cross that tree. 'Kay?"

"Got it."

It was barely five meters. She bolted, and then she stopped. It really went that fast. We did that a few times.

"How was that?"

"Uh, one second exactly," I said.

"You said that last time. You know you have to push the button to make it go, right?"

"I know how a stopwatch works. Most normal people can't time things down to the millisecond."

"Well, try harder." Yakishio grinned at me before pulling her shirt up to wipe her face. She paid no mind to her exposed midriff. "I'm feeling pretty winded, honestly. Break time?"

"Didn't know you got tired."

"Hey, I'm only human. You do know that, right?"

First a full Yanami, now a tired Yakishio. The last twenty-four hours had been full of surprises.

Yakishio weaved around the trees toward the main sanctuary of the shrine.

"Pretty deserted," she said. "I've never been here this late."

She passed through a couple of torii gates, then turned and waved at me. I followed, not entirely confident I wouldn't be isekai'd upon making it to the other side.

She sat down on a bench and patted the space next to her. I acquiesced, taking the opposite side.

"I'm gonna go out on a limb and assume you came here to... What're you doing all the way over there?"

"I, uh..."

Yakishio scooched over to my end. "We don't have to cuddle. The distance just stings a little, that's all." I apologized, for what it was worth. "Don't sweat it. So, you came to talk, I'm guessing."

"Surprise," I said weakly. "I get it, y'know, but you had us scared for a while, ghosting us like that."

"Sorry. I run when I get flustered. Bad habit." She looked so fragile as she turned her gaze up. "I really did mean to take it to the grave with me. But I went and screwed that up, and I didn't know what to do anymore."

I couldn't fault her. Even if she had intended to lay it all bare one day, that wasn't the time or place. I understood the urge to run.

"I figured I'd let time do its thing, y'know," she continued. "And then eventually things could go back to normal."

"They won't."

Her best friend now knew she wanted to be something more. Things would change. Their outings together not least of all.

"Do you think maybe Mitsuki and I can't be friends anymore?" Yakishio pleaded with me with her eyes. "I'll never come between them. I really mean that."

I forced myself not to give in to sympathy and shook my head. "You've been meeting with him in private, Yakishio. With Ayano. I saw."

"Y-you—" Yanami zipped up onto her feet. "I-I wasn't—it wasn't what it—"

I held my hands out like I was placating a wild animal. It usually worked on Kaju. "It's okay. I know. You were just giving him advice."

"Oh, great. So you know everything." She dropped back onto the bench. A sad, broken laugh escaped her. "Cat's out of the bag. Don't I feel stupid." She scratched her cheek. "Yana-chan?"

"She knows. Komari's probably picked up on it and Tsukinoki-senpai definitely knows."

"Even Komari-chan, huh?"

"It's all out in the open now, Yakishio. It's unreasonable to expect things to stay the same."

"I know. I know that."

She kept her head down for a while, deciding what to say next.

"Mitsuki's not sure what exactly he and Asagumo-san are," she finally said. She picked up a rock and chucked it. The darkness swallowed it up without a sound. "His first girlfriend and all. He doesn't know how to reciprocate, *what* to reciprocate, how any of it works, really."

"Okay, but like, why was he going to you in the first place? It's private. No one asks girls how to be intimate with them. Besides, you don't wanna hear about any of that, do you?"

Yakishio waved me off. "Come on, we're in high school. They're dating. They're gonna do that stuff." I was shocked to hear she'd come to terms with it. In any case, she was right. High school couples would do as high school couples do. Hakamada × Himemiya could attest to that. "I'm sure they've already held hands by now. Before long they'll—"

"Yakishio, you know they've straight up made out already, right?"

That hit her like a punch to the gut. Almost literally, by the look of it. She did not, in fact, know.

"They... So they kiss now. Okay."

How was it possible that, even though we were separated by more than half a prefecture, Ayano was still screwing me over? Why had he picked *that* aspect specifically to keep to himself?

"Well, uh, they're dating, right? They're gonna do that stuff," I echoed.

"But that fast? It's a little fast, right?"

"You really think *I* have an answer to that question?"

"Fair point." Everyone was so quick to forget who they were talking to. "But you're right. They're dating..." She buried her face in her legs. "You're right. I hate that you're right."

"Here's what I think, Yakishio. You're going to keep making the same mistakes if you try and go right back to being all buddy-buddy again."

"I know."

"I'm not saying you have to stop being friends, but you do have to acknowledge that concessions are going to have to be made."

"I know. I get it. That's why I tried to *just* be a friend and hear him out. I really did try. I told him to communicate and be upfront and all that like a good friend should. I really thought I was coming to terms with everything. That I was doing things right." She sat upright again. "But then I started to care about how I looked."

I didn't follow. Wasn't that normal for a girl and her crush? "I don't see anything wrong with that."

She shook her head. "You know how I'm always a sweaty mess after practice? I usually wouldn't care and just head straight home. But when my meetings with Mitsuki started, I couldn't do that anymore. It wasn't like I could get super dressed up or anything though, right? So I started going home to clean up first, come back, and then pretend I was right off the track. If I didn't have time to do that, I made sure to keep spare clothes in the club room."

Yakishio closed her eyes and smiled, remembering. I could feel her joy, the fun they must have had together.

When she opened her eyes again, the smile was gone. "It was never supposed to be anything other than that. I only wanted to hear him out. Give advice. But I was just so happy being with him, and I... I didn't want to stop." Her lip trembled. She clenched her fists. "There was one time. One time I had this awful thought."

"What kind of thought?"

"I hate to even say it. I..." Her voice was barely a rasp. "I wished they would break up."

I opened my mouth to say something but closed it again. The Yanami I didn't recognize came back to me. Her words.

She has no reason not to take what she wants.

Yakishio bit down on her lip, trying her hardest to keep the dam from bursting. "Mitsuki came to me for help, and I..." She wrapped her arms around herself. "I'm terrible. I'm a bad person." The first tear fell. The rest came easily. "I didn't... I didn't mean to..." And then she sobbed. "I'm sorry... I'm sorry." She wailed and cried like a lost child.

And I could only sit there.

But I was there for her. Because I could do nothing else.

Someday, Yakishio would forget what happened tonight, our conversation becoming a blur among a cascade of other memories. But I swore to myself I'd remember. I'd never forget the things she felt that night.

***

Minutes came and went while Yakishio's sobs eventually became snivels.

She wiped her eyes with the back of her hand. "Sorry for dumping all that on you."

"Doesn't bother me. Sorry for putting you on the spot."

Yakishio shook her head. Laughed a bit. "That's the second time I've looked stupid in front of you." She smiled, tears still resting in her eyes. "Don't tell anyone I cried, okay?"

I smiled back. "Sure. After you hear one last thing I have to say."

"Blackmail, eh? All right. Lay it on me."

I cleared my throat. "It's about a friend of mine."

"*You* have friends?"

Unrelated.

"I do, as a matter of fact. So this friend is kind of in the same boat as you. She's got a friend who already has a girlfriend."

"Okay."

"And she's totally supportive and isn't making any moves or anything, but..."

"But?"

"But...she'd totally jump on him if she thought for even a second that she had a shot. At least, I think she would."

"She'd *what*?! Nukkun, she sounds like trouble! Are you friends with trouble?!"

Some would say so, yes.

"But the thing is, she's not out to ruin things between them," I clarified. "She's trying to make things work despite things being as they are and set healthy boundaries. She *is* making an effort. As much as she can without invalidating the way she still feels about her friend."

"That's super deep and all, but you did just say she'd steal someone's boyfriend if she could." That she would. "I'm not sure I get why you're telling me this."

I looked up and wondered that myself. "Y'know, let's just say you're sweeter than you give yourself credit for."

Yakishio looked up too. "I guess. That does make me feel a little better."

I offered a silent thanks to the hater for being a perfect example.

Yakishio rested her hands behind her and leaned back. "I feel lucky to have you guys, you know. People who won't leave me even when I screw up."

"It's because we know, trust, and ultimately care about you."

"Huh." She gave me a look. "You're being awfully nice today. You get a cat recently or something?"

"It's late. The brain goes weird places when it's late. Ignore me."

It was well past normal thought hours. I caught myself glancing around for a certain hater who would have loved the new teasing material.

"What?" Yakishio asked.

"Nothing. We should get back before Yanami starts to worry."

"Oh, yikes, she's up, huh? Now I feel bad."

I stood, beating the dirt off the back of my pants. Yakishio started to do the same before suddenly sitting back down.

"Yo." She held her arms out to me.

"What? There a bug or..." I paused. Then snorted and offered my hands.

Yakishio graciously accepted, pulling herself up. "You're learning."

"It's late." I started to hurry away.

She quickly caught up. "Hey, Nukkun."

"Hm?"

"I'll talk to Mitsuki and Asagumo-san," she said. "Promise."

"Asagumo-san too?"

"Yeah. I *was* sneaking around with her boyfriend behind her back. Feel like I owe her an apology."

I considered telling Yakishio that Asagumo-san kind of maybe already knew that but decided against it. The more they communicated with their own words, the better.

"I think you should," I said. "Want me to let her know you want to talk? She's been crazy worried about you."

"Yeah. Thanks. I'm good with whenever she's free." I had high hopes things would go well after our talk. "Also, there's, um, one other thing I want your help with." She cast her eyes down nervously.

"Sure. What do you need?"

"I-I'm just a little scared, I guess. About seeing Mitsuki again. I might run away again if someone's not there to keep my head on straight, so, um..." She gripped my shirt and yanked it. "I want you to be there! Not that you need to baby me or anything. It's just, having someone around would make it easier. I, um... I know I'm not really in a position to ask or anything, but I—"

"Yeah, sure. That's fine."

Yakishio's jaw hung in the air. "Wait, for real? Just like that? You're cool with it?"

"I'm not downplaying the situation or anything. I'm just like..."

"You're like what?"

"Why not, y'know?"

"Oh. Lame. I was expecting something cooler."

"Look, one-liners aren't easy to improvise, okay?"

She put a hand on her hip and let out a dramatic sigh. "That's your problem right there, Nukkun." And then she turned on her heel and sauntered away.

"That right where?" I grumbled.

Yakishio whipped back around and flashed her trademark toothy grin. "Figure it out."

She hurried on.

***

Yanami collected her empty breakfast plates with dreary, barely opened eyes.

"Ugh... How are you awake right now, Nukumizu-kun?"

"I fell asleep pretty much as soon as I got back." I smeared the last of the marmalade onto the last of my toast. Grandma Yakishio had hit it out of the park with that stuff. "Rough night?"

"I don't even know what time it was when I finally went back to sleep. Man, I'm so sleepy I barely ate." She let out a yawn. I gave her the benefit of the doubt and assumed she was too tired to remember to cover her mouth. Also, by "barely ate," she meant at least three whole slices of toast.

Yanami had been waiting for us outside when Yakishio and I got back last night. They exchanged like two or three words max, giggled a bit, and then went right back to their room, playfully poking and prodding each other. All I remembered was being too tired to even change back into my pajamas before collapsing into bed.

Much more recent in my memory was Yakishio practically yanking me out of it this morning.

"Hey, Komari-chan, do you want more salad?" asked Yakishio. "You've barely even touched your toast."

"I-I don't eat much in the morning... It's too early."

Speaking of, Yakishio was clearly spirited enough to pester Komari, who was making a valiant effort to finish off the remaining half of her bread. Her good mood felt more genuine this time. Maybe it was conceited of me, but I liked to think our talk had something to do with that.

I sipped my tea. Their exchanges always made for good entertainment. Then I noticed Yanami staring at me.

"Hey, where'd you get that shirt?" she asked me.

"Oh, I'm just borrowing it. Gotta clean it and give it back sometime."

Yakishio gave up on Komari long enough to chime in, "Yeah, that one's mine. Glad it fits okay."

"It's yours? Wait, seriously? Should I take it off? I'll take it off."

I'd assumed it was her grandfather's. Sure, it was clean, but women's clothes were still women's clothes.

"Nah, it's nothin' special. I tried to give that to Yana-chan yesterday, but it was too sma—"

"Lemon-chan!" Yanami snapped. I finished the sentence in my head. "I literally told you not to tell anyone!"

"It's just Nukumizu," said Yakishio. "That's fine, right?"

"Not anymore it's not!"

Those two had no concept of a quiet morning. I downed the last of my tea and gathered my plates.

As I stood to put them away, my mind wandered to the fabric hanging from my shoulders. They were broader than Yanami's, so that couldn't have been what made it too small for her. Only one point of variability logically remained: the chest region.

My mind wandered its way into the gutter. I attempted to salvage some composure by thinking of Kaju. It worked.

Just then, an arm slithered around my shoulder. "Wassup, Romeo?" Tsukinoki-senpai purred. "You have a good time last night?"

"Stop breathing in my ear," I said. "Also, let me go."

There went my composure all over again.

"Looks to me like whatever you did worked. You've got moves after all."

"I didn't..." I started to act humble but cut myself off. "Our job's just to be there for her. Now get off me, please."

Senpai ruffled my hair. "Aww, look at him get all flustered. I've still got it."

"Y-you'll go for anyone, w-won't you, Nukumizu?" Komari looked at me like I was human garbage. So only mildly more aggressively than normal.

"How do you *not* see that I'm the one being harassed right now? What is this?" Now, this was the kind of slander that ended careers.

I detached from the chaos, just as Yakishio's grandma strolled over with a teapot. "Would you like more tea, Nukumizu-kun?"

"I'm okay, thank you," I replied.

She nodded, then turned to Yakishio and the others laughing and giggling together. "She's got good friends."

"Depending on your definition of 'good,' I guess. The girls of the lit club are nothing if not unique, and not always in a good way."

"I was including you, you know." She pounded me on the back and went to go join her granddaughter. Now I knew where Yakishio got her violent expressions of affection.

I continued on my way to actually put these dishes down.

Too Many Losing Heroines!

Central Japan Railway—Hon-Nagashino Station

A YOUNG GIRL WITH SUN-KISSED SKIN ALIGHTED from the SUV at Hon-Nagashino Station, along the Iida Line.

"Thanks, Grandma. I'll let you know when I get home."

Yakishio Lemon waved to the elderly woman in the driver seat.

Her grandmother leaned out the window and smiled at her granddaughter. "Why don't I take you all the way back, sweetie?"

"That's okay. Need some time to think anyway."

"All right. Well, be careful now."

"I will." Lemon circled around and hugged her through the window.

Four days ago, Lemon had scared her grandmother about half to death when she arrived out of the blue. Twice over when she saw the robotic smile her granddaughter had plastered onto her face.

It was gone now, replaced by something real. Something a little more grown-up, the grandmother thought. Then again, a grandma's eyes always measured in maturity when it came to grandkids.

The grandmother straightened the clip in Lemon's hair. "You've been blessed with wonderful people in your life."

"Yeah. Guess I have."

Another hug, and off she went. With one last wave, Lemon vanished into the station.

She strode past an empty waiting room and its many dull brown seats, then through the ticket gate. There were no employees out at this hour. She crossed over the crossing and went to where a few scattered people waited for their trains.

Lemon patted herself on the cheeks. No more running.

Her friends in the literature club should have been well on their way back to Toyohashi right about then. Lemon wanted to do right by them. To settle things for good between her and Mitsuki.

Hon-Nagashino to Toyohashi was about an hour by train. Lemon scanned the platform for her gate when she spotted something that made her heart skip a beat. A girl in an orange one-piece and a fancy hat stood not too far from her.

Lemon pressed her hand to her chest and breathed before approaching. "Asagumo-san?"

"I suppose this is the first time it's been just the two of us," she said, lowering her head.

Lemon wanted to ask what she was doing here, but that would have been redundant. Why else if not for the obvious?

Instead, she asked, "How did you know I'd be here?"

"Nukumizu-san said you wanted to talk, so I asked him for your schedule."

"No idea how you sussed out I'd be at *this* station. You could have waited for me in Toyohashi."

"This couldn't wait. Besides, I wanted to talk too." Asagumo removed her hat, tilted her head ever so slightly to look at her, and smiled. "I want to get to know you, Yakishio-san. May I?"

There was fear and anxiety in those words. Beyond the pretty face she put on.

Lemon lowered the last of her walls. "Yeah. I'd like that."

The tracks rumbled, telling of a coming train as a speaker announced its arrival. "Toyohashi-bound," it said. The two girls, one tawny, one short, watched it pull up to the platform.

"Train's here," said Lemon.

"So it seems," said the short one. "Should we take it together or let it go and continue this in the waiting room?"

"What's your plan if you miss this one?"

"Take the next one."

"At least we'd have each other, I guess."

They laughed together.

The train's brakes creaked gently. When it came to a stop, Asagumo pushed the button to open the door. "After you. It's a long wait to the next one."

"Why thank you, Asagumo-san."

"You're very welcome." Asagumo started to follow but turned around at the last second, hiked her skirt, and scurried back.

"What are you doing?"

"One second!" she shouted back. She dunked something into the trash can then hopped back onto the train. As the doors shut, she let out a sigh.

"What was that about?"

"Just a promise to Nukumizu-san that I broke. I'm done now, though. For good."

Lemon blinked her big eyes. "A whuh?"

Asagumo made a playful grin and put a finger up to her lips. "Keep it between us, okay?"

Lemon couldn't help but grin back.

People can never truly understand one another. That's why we communicate, to try and make sense of the nonsense. To know the unknowable.

For the first time in her life, Lemon truly and genuinely wanted to know Asagumo.

LOSS 4

Yakishio Lemon Tells All

THE NEXT NIGHT, I WAS BROWSING THE LIGHT NOVELS at Seibunkan. Tsukinoki-senpai had made yesterday's trip back from Shinshiro fly by with her nonstop chitchat.

I wanted to close the book on everything the second I got home, but I knew there was one more chapter left—Yakishio and Ayano still had to have their talk. My job was to see Yakishio safely to their meeting spot tonight. I had left home a little early, too antsy to sit still until it was time.

One thing about this meeting: Yakishio wasn't going for pity points or to shoot her shot one last time. She'd already done that. This was more like a post-mortem sort of deal. What it would reveal was anyone's guess.

"Oh, hey. New volume of HSG."

HSG was, of course, the colloquial title for *My Apartment Came with a High School Girl and Now I Can't Afford to Eat*—a story about a girl who bums with the protagonist and the hyper-realistic financial strain that comes with taking care of dependents. Most recently, another girl had joined the duo, thus forcing the protagonist to take even more drastic measures to make ends meet.

"Whoa, he takes up newspaper delivery?" I had to check this out.

Someone tapped me on the shoulder while I read the back blurb. "Figured I'd find you here, Nukkun."

"Oh. Yakishio."

There was the woman of the hour.

"I tried your house, but I heard you went to the station," she said. "Had a hunch."

"Oh. Cool. But, uh, what's with the getup?"

She had on a running shirt and a pair of shorts. Hardly the attire of typical bookstore clientele.

"I was runnin'," she said. "Also, since when am I *not* dressed like this?" She smiled proudly.

"You sure, though? That's how you wanna see Ayano?"

"Yup. I wanna be myself when I do it." She studied the shelf in front of me. "So these are those 'light novel' things. Think I could manage one?"

"I mean, they're easy reads. Don't see why not."

"I haven't even started on the book report. Which one of these is the shortest?"

"Yakishio, tomorrow is the last day of summer vacation."

"Pro tip, all you gotta do is say you left it at home and you get a free extra week. Heck, sometimes you'll get lucky and the teacher'll forget all about it." Yakishio reached for one. "Oh, hey, this one looks neat."

I shook my head. "I wouldn't. The protagonist streaks through town in literally the first few pages."

"What about this?"

"Nope. MC gets mounted by a half-naked, eight-hundred-year-old little girl in the first color illustration."

"I'm genuinely making an effort to pick out the most normal-sounding ones here."

"It's genuinely impressive how terribly you're doing."

I told her I'd lend her an easy one to knock out her report, and then we left. We stepped out into the streetlight-illuminated, not-quite dark of night.

Yakishio stretched. "Nothin' like a good book to get the brain juices flowing, am I right?"

Imagine how it'll feel to actually read one, I quipped to myself.

We still had some time to kill. Originally, the plan had been to convene near Yakishio's place, then head straight to meet Ayano from there. I peeked at my watch.

Yakishio grabbed my arm and stole a peek too. "Whatcha gonna do? Walk?"

"I was gonna burn a bit more time and then take the tram, personally."

"Hm," she hummed, dissatisfied. She scraped the bottom of her shoe against the pavement. "Ah, well. Guess I'll run a bit more, then meet up with you again."

"Yeah, let's just do that. Stick to the plan."

Yakishio didn't seem sold. On second thought, she *had* come all the way out here just to see me.

I scratched at the back of my head and stared off into nothing. "But I guess I'd get there right on time if I walked. I *could* use the exercise."

Yakishio copied my tone. "And I *could* use a breather after all that reading. Walking *would* be a good way to stretch my legs."

We glanced at each other at the same time. We shared a snicker.

"We *are* going the same way and all," I said.

"Very true. We *are*. I guess I'll just *have* to go with you then."

Yakishio held her hands behind her head and gave me a snide look. I countered it with a just-as-snide grin.

***

Forty minutes of small talk went by. We talked about summer homework, the opening ceremony in two days, a senpai on Yakishio's track team who was just a little bit scary. Over time, though, the pauses got longer. Her comments got shorter.

They were meeting at their old elementary school, and we were almost there.

I studied the building through the fence as we walked its perimeter. "Lights are off."

Wait, this was totally trespassing. I'd only just realized.

"Almost time." Yakishio held her chest and breathed. She muttered an encouraging something to herself. "All right."

"Hey, so, it might be a little late to mention this, but are you allowed to just walk into elementary schools? I feel like that's not allowed."

"Yeah, you could have mentioned that earlier."

I refused to be blamed for that.

She put a hand on her hip and tutted. "It's open during the day. It'll be fine so long as we don't cause a scene or anything. Trust me, I'm used to this."

A repeat offender. At least it wasn't my butt on the line. As I started to raise my arm in farewell, Yakishio prodded it. "You said that on purpose to take my mind off things, didn't you?" she said.

"Uh, no?"

"Thanks. I'm okay now. You wait for me here."

Apparently, my job was round-trip. Good to know, though I wasn't thrilled about the idea of standing around here in the dead of night.

Yakishio took note of my sketchy fidgeting and raised an eyebrow. "You're not about to tell me you'd leave a girl to walk home this late all by herself, are you?"

"Psh. Me? No way."

"Good. See you in a bit." She gave one of her trademark grins then raised her hand. It took me about five turns of the ol' brain gears to realize what the gesture meant and raise my hand as well. "It ends tonight!" She gave me five with all the force to make up for how long I'd kept her waiting.

She was off like a lightning bolt, hurdling the back gate with an ease that spoke to more than one offense.

***

The moonlit courtyard was smaller than Lemon remembered. Back then, everything was so new, every nook an unexplored piece of the world. Back then, "small" was hardly a word in her vocabulary.

Lemon walked through the old playground, feeling the nostalgic sting of cold metal against her fingers as she passed shrunken playthings. The quiet emptiness made her uncomfortable. She found herself wishing for morning.

She searched the campus for him, and there at the edge, in front of a white Stevenson screen, she found him. A tall, anxiously shuffling young man.

Her world turned. What was up threatened to become down. Lemon breathed, fighting against the instinct to flee, and approached. Every step was a victory.

When she stopped in front of him, she realized she hadn't actually thought about what she would say. How she would act.

She half settled on a smile. "Thanks for coming, Mitsuki."

"It's important."

It was deeper now, obscured beneath years of maturity, but Lemon knew and recognized the voice. She recognized the way he pursed his lip when he was nervous. It relieved her to know she wasn't the only one. He was as lost as she was.

"Feels like it's been a lifetime since we've been here, huh?" Lemon turned, inviting him to walk.

Mitsuki followed half a step behind. "Four years for me."

"Then four for me too." Lemon remembered lots of tears at graduation, thinking she would come back to play here all the time since she lived so close and then never actually doing it.

She jogged up to a jungle gym with a slide attached, admiring it.

"You're gonna hurt yourself. It's dark," Mitsuki admonished.

"I'm not getting on it. I'm not a kid anymore." She pouted her lips, frustrated that he'd spoiled her fun so quickly. "Remember when we used to get on the swings together and see who could jump off the farthest?"

"I remember *you* doing that, and nearly breaking your leg in the process."

"Maybe. Whoa, this tire takes me back." Lemon hopped onto one of the half-buried tires in the ground. No one actually knew what they were for. Some rode them, some crawled through them, some jumped over them. Lemon hopped across them, plopping down on the last one. "Were they always so small?"

"Pretty sure," said Mitsuki. "I don't remember you playing with them much the last couple of years we were here." He sat down on a tire next to her.

That made Lemon smile. That really was enough for her. She savored the feeling. Because it was probably the last night she'd ever get to feel it.

"We met in second grade, right?" she finally said, as much as it pained her to end the moment. Mitsuki nodded. "I didn't actually like you at first, y'know. All you ever did was read books, and I just didn't get it."

That was news to Mitsuki. He took it with a wry smile. "I got it into my head that I had to read everything in the class library for whatever reason."

"Do you...? Nah. You probably don't remember the first time we talked, do you?"

"It was when you hurt your foot."

It was the fall of second grade. Lemon had sprained her ankle jumping off of the swing set, and though it wasn't anything serious, she had been strictly told no rough-housing. An abundance of free time and boredom had been the start of their relationship.

"You do remember." Lemon chuckled.

"How could I forget the day the queen troublemaker made it her business to interrupt my reading time? It was traumatic, I tell you."

"Gee, tell me how you really feel! You seriously mean you didn't just read to me because you felt bad for the sad, lonely girl who couldn't go out and play?"

"It was less reading and more summarizing. You never had the attention span."

"Right, that did happen. You pretty much just gave me the digest." Lemon giggled. Mitsuki stopped playing at exasperation and laughed with her. "I never got books. They always made me sleepy. But whenever you talked about them, for some reason, I never felt that way."

Mitsuki hummed in acknowledgment.

"That's why I kept coming back, even after I got better." That was when the excuses started. It was raining, it was too hot, too cold—Lemon found any reason she could to join in on whatever he was up to.

"Little did I know, I'd have to explain the entire plot of every *Harry Potter* book to you one day," Mitsuki bemoaned, though not without a smile.

"Oh, *you* wanna complain? Imagine how confused I was when I saw the movies! You told me Harry marries Hermione in the end!"

"I didn't think you'd actually believe me."

"Great, so I'm just dumb then."

Mitsuki burst out laughing. Lemon started to argue, but she couldn't hold it in either.

She wiped the corner of her eye while she caught her breath. "Good times."

"Hard to believe it's been eight years."

They could have kept reminiscing long into the night. How Lemon wanted to. But dawn would come regardless, and it was up to her whether she would be awake to see it.

Lemon took the reins and said, "Remember in junior high, when I said I wanted to go to Tsuwabuki and everyone laughed at me? Even the teachers. Pretty harsh, huh?"

"It did sound pretty insane with your grades."

"You didn't laugh, though."

"But I *did* think you were crazy."

"Wait a minute, that's right! You didn't laugh, but you *did* tell me pigs would fly before I made it through general admissions!" Lemon shot Mitsuki an accusatory glare. "You were literally like, 'Go for a sponsor and pray.'"

"In my defense, your grades were pretty much in the pits."

Tsuwabuki High School was particularly distinguished in Aichi Prefecture. One that might as well have been a pipe dream for Lemon at the time.

"Okay, so why did you help me then?"

"Well, why wouldn't I help out a friend?"

Lemon flinched at the word. "Friends" was what they were. What they always would be.

"Awful lot of work to do for just a friend," she managed. "You even taught me how to prioritize questions and maximize points and stuff. How do you even learn stuff like that?"

Mitsuki's lessons had extended beyond the standard periodical quiz. He had gone to great lengths to learn the key points in every subject, right down to the idiosyncrasies of what specific teachers would be looking for, all to bump Lemon's grades up to meet Tsuwabuki's specific requirements for sponsored students.

"What can I say? I was a teacher's pet. I probably could have made a decent guidance counselor back then."

"Okay, but you literally wrote down all their birthdays and wedding anniversaries and everything. That's a *lot* of work."

"I'm an all or nothing kind of guy," Mitsuki said. "That said, track was all you. You were team captain, and you stood up on that winner's podium at the prefectural meet." Although it had been he who suggested she shoot for both, on account of the fact that the next national inter-high would be held locally. "Also, don't forget, you studied your butt off. By the time we were third years, you were one of the top students."

"Top for our school," Lemon corrected. "I was below average on the mock exams."

The latter half of their junior high years had been a three-legged race with the two of them scrambling to make it in time for entrance exams. To an outsider, Lemon may have appeared superhuman, juggling so much along with track practice, but she knew what she had gone through to manage it. What *they* had gone through.

She held that shared suffering close to her heart.

"I just don't get it," she said, bending over like something was driving her crazy.

"You don't get what?"

"Everything. All the crap you did for me when you had your own junk to worry about," Lemon snapped. "*Would* you do that for 'just a friend'?"

Mitsuki furrowed his brow. "You told me that your family was full of scholars and lawyers. That you felt bad not being as smart as them. That's why you wanted to go to Tsuwabuki."

"I'm surprised you remember so much." That didn't escape Lemon's notice. "Yeah, both my mom and dad...and pretty much everyone in my family went to really good schools. They always told me not to compare myself to them, but sometimes you can't help it." She sat back upright, bracing herself. "That's only half-true, though."

Mitsuki sensed the gravity of her tone, so unlike the Lemon he knew.

Lemon faced him squarely. "I just wanted to go to school with you."

He met her gaze, forgetting to breathe. "Lemon..."

"I was honest with you, Mitsuki. Now it's your turn."

"My turn?"

"Why did you do all that for me? I want the truth."

Mitsuki clasped his hands together. There would be no running for either of them that night. "I...wanted to go to school with you too," he said to the ground. "You were already making waves in junior high, winning races, always getting recognized for something at assemblies. Everyone loved you. You were the center of every room you walked in."

He breathed deep, picking his next words. "I felt like I was losing you, so I was relieved when you asked for my help. And I was, well, ecstatic when you said you wanted to go to the same school as me."

Mitsuki opened and closed his mouth several more times. He had more to say but didn't know how to say it. Eventually, he stopped trying.

Lemon broke the silence. "That's the first time I've ever heard you say that."

"I was so caught up in the moment back then. There were so many emotions, and I just couldn't pin down that the one that mattered most was..."

Mitsuki didn't finish the sentence. He couldn't. Not anymore. But he didn't need to.

"I'll say it for you."

Mitsuki flinched. Lemon only smiled and, in the softest of voices, said the unsayable:

"You loved me."

Silence louder than words. It was the only answer Mitsuki could hope to give.

Calmly, he started to speak again. "I never knew what that meant to me until..." Hesitation.

"You can say it," Lemon urged.

"Until Chihaya. The things I felt for her, the way my heart flutters when we're together—that was when I realized." A realization eight years too late for Lemon. "That was when I learned that that's how it feels to be in love." And yet a realization eight years in the making for Asagumo Chihaya.

"I'm glad," she said quietly. Their time together had had a purpose. She smiled at Mitsuki. "I really am."

"But I..."

"I mean it. The person I love said they loved me back. I'm happy. As happy as I can be."

As happy as I can be without being with you.

Lemon refused to give form to those thoughts. Their time was over before it had even begun. An undisclosed game of love, lost in the first round.

She forced herself to keep smiling. "So what made you fall for her?"

"Are you...sure you want me to say?"

"The genie's out of the bottle, buddy." Lemon laughed.

"I..." He spoke slowly. "I want to work with books in the future."

"For real?" Lemon blurted. "Like, publishing, or are you gonna be an author?"

"It's not really that specific yet. Just a dream I have." Mitsuki looked down at his open hand. "I still have to take stock of the things I know I can do versus the things I specifically *want* to do.

Either way, I'd like to go and study at a university in Tokyo. See what I can do with my four years there."

Lemon lost herself in him for a while. In the future he looked to. She figured there was only one reason he was talking about this now. "And Asagumo-san's the same?"

"Yeah. Same dream, more or less. Rather, she's the one who set me on the path to begin with."

"Wow. I could never do what you guys do."

"Right back at you, Lemon."

Fair enough, she thought.

She stared up at the sky with Mitsuki and pointed. "Hey, why's that one so bright? Is that the North Star?"

"The North Star's that way. My guess is you're looking at the Summer Triangle. See the other two? Those are each of the points."

"All I'm seein' is one. It's sorta red. Maybe it's Mars?"

Mitsuki squinted and nodded. "Antares, I think. That's the Scorpio constellation."

"Scorpio. Neat." It saddened Lemon a little, the way they saw different things in the same sky. She thought of Asagumo Chihaya. She would have seen the same stars. "You be good to her, y'hear? You need a girl like Asagumo-san to keep you in line."

"I know."

There was silence again. Neither had any more words to end it with. What needed to be said had been said, and now someone had to be left with the unfortunate task of wrapping it up all nice.

"Let's go, Lemon." Mitsuki stood, taking the role upon himself.

"I'm gonna stick around here a while longer. Could use some alone time."

"You gonna be okay?"

Lemon nodded. She would be. In time. "Just taking five. I'll be back to my old self before you know it. Just you wait."

***

I'd been waiting for Yakishio to finish trespassing for about twenty minutes.

"Maybe I did find a cat today." I squinted past the gate she'd vaulted over. I had a story all prepared for if anyone asked what we were doing here, and it involved a runaway feline. "She'll be a tortoiseshell and her name will be Nyaruko."

I imagined Nyaruko as an ex-stray who would only respond to or take food from me. She was, of course, a girl in the event that she polymorphed into a human one day. I started scrolling through images on my phone, just to be prepared.

That was when I noticed someone standing in front of me. "Uh, meow?!"

"What're you doing here, Nukumizu?"

It was Ayano. I hadn't even noticed him cross back over the gate.

"I'm the, uh, chauffeur," I said.

"Mine?"

Dude.

I cleared my throat, finally switching gears into social mode.

"I'm walking Yakishio back home." I peered around him at the school. "She still there?"

"Yeah. She said she wanted some time to herself." He picked up on my shuffling and read my mind. "Don't worry. It was a good talk. Thanks for being here for her."

I decided to trust the placid look on his face for once. "Least I can do is make sure she gets home okay."

Ayano didn't budge. I glanced at him, and our eyes met.

"Chihaya told me you don't actually have a crush on Yanami-san," he said.

"Well, uh..." That whole story had slipped my mind entirely.

He considered me for a while. "You're a good guy, Nukumizu."

"No idea what gave you that idea."

"Just something I've learned recently. Apparently, it's a pretty rare thing to have a friend who's willing to stick their neck out for you."

Friend? Who was he talking about? "I'm not her friend, if that's what you're implying."

"What? You're joking, right?"

"I mean, neither of us have actually *said* that we're friends. Like, officially and all," I rambled. "I mean, if *she* thinks we're friends, great, but like, I mean, we've never really established it, so how can I assume, y'know?"

The last day of the semester before summer break came back to me. My friendship with Yanami had apparently begun under my nose, without my knowledge. World-shattering as that knowledge was to me at the time, I did consider myself capable of growth as a human being.

"Not that you absolutely *need* a verbal confirmation to be friends, that is," I corrected myself. "I know that."

"Good. You had me worried there."

"What I was trying to say is, you could potentially assume you're closer than you actually are, and you can think you're friends when they don't actually think the same. Imagine how embarrassing that would be."

"Honestly, I think you've gotten a bit stuck in your own head, Nukumizu." Ayano started to laugh it off but turned serious all of a sudden. "No. No, you may have a point in a certain sense."

Finally, someone understood. I nodded enthusiastically. "Exactly. The confirmation process has merit."

"I see where you're coming from, but you're overthinking the kind of person Lemon is. Also, we're friends, aren't we? And we never had to spell it out explicitly."

"We're friends?"

Ayano recoiled. "Ouch. You're killing me here."

He was serious? Wait. I had to think about this. Maybe it was fine? I didn't actively hate the guy or anything.

"All right, well, uh, better late than never," I said. "Here's to our future together?"

"I'm not proposing to you, dude," Ayano cackled. I laughed with him.

Last time, I was the proposer. This time, the proposee. That was a pretty funny coincidence, I had to admit.

Amidst our hearty laughter appeared a tawny girl on the other side of the school gate, and she did not look amused. "Well, I *was* feeling sentimental," she said, cheery, nonetheless. She hopped over the gate. "What're you two dorks up to?"

"Guy stuff." Ayano nudged me with his elbow.

I clumsily nudged him back. "Yeah, uh, what he said."

Was I doing this right? Did that look natural? I might have been overselling it.

Ayano put his hand on my shoulder. "Your chauffeur awaits, Lemon."

"Yeah, yeah. Hold in those tears on your way home, princess, 'cause I'm not coming to save you," Yakishio said.

Was Ayano leaving her? Just like that? I supposed he couldn't put Asagumo-san through any more unspecified outings after all this.

Yakishio came up and smacked me on the back. "Sorry for the wait, Nukkun. Let's get going."

"Yeah. Sure." I watched Ayano turn to leave. My brain buzzed with a thousand conflicting thoughts best acknowledged. I ignored all of them. "Actually, just a sec. Sorry."

"Huh?"

I snatched Ayano's arm and dragged him somewhere Yakishio couldn't overhear. "What're you doing, Nukumizu?"

"Why not walk with her? One last time?"

He stiffened. "We had our talk. I don't want to do that to Chihaya."

"I get that, but don't overthink it. What's a few more minutes together?"

"I don't know about this."

He and I looked back at Yakishio. She was peering at us curiously a ways away.

"You're just walking her home," I pressed. "Is that so wrong?"

"I told Chihaya we were going to have a talk, but anything more than that..."

"Might make you a cheater. Yeah."

Ayano thought about that for a while before grinning in surrender. "Don't tell her."

"Don't do anything that'll make me have to." I shoved him toward Yakishio. "She's all yours."

"Nukkun? What's going on?" she asked.

"I've got an errand to run, so Ayano's gonna sub in for me."

Yakishio jolted upright like she'd been struck by a lightning bolt.

Ayano shuffled up to her, awkwardly scratching at his head. "It's late, so, uh, you mind if I walk you home?"

Yakishio nodded meekly. "Sure."

As I watched them go, I noticed Ayano wasn't wearing that bracelet his girlfriend had given him. I shrugged it off. "He's as ditzy as they come."

It was a special night. The sort that turns sweet girls just a little bit sour. Regardless of the fact that Asagumo-san probably would have been on my side in this, they deserved this one secret between themselves.

I started on my way home alone.

"Hey, Mitsuki."

"Yeah?"

"I love you."

"Lemon..."

"What?"

"Nothing. Thanks. It means a lot to hear that."

"Heh... Hey, can I say something I probably shouldn't?"

"What kind of something?"

"The kind that Asagumo-san doesn't have to know about, and then I'll never ask for anything ever again."

Mitsuki saw himself reflected in Lemon's bright brown eyes. He nodded. Just one secret.

Yakishio Lemon parted her lips. They told all.

Too Many Losing Heroines!

EPILOGUE

After Happily Ever After

TWO UNEVENTFUL DAYS LATER, AND THE NEW semester was upon us.

"It's over..." I sighed as I headed for the front door.

Summer vacation was finally over. As was waking up without an alarm, cycling through video games and manga in the morning, spending the afternoon reading light novels or watching airing anime, doing the obligatory bare minimum of homework right before bed, and otherwise idling the days away in blessed air conditioning.

I had to do a triple take at the date on my phone this morning before I believed it.

"It is what it is," I told myself.

I checked myself in the mirror in our front hallway. Same old uniform. Same old haircut. The bedhead could have used a little work.

"Leaving already, Oniisama?" Kaju pitter-pattered over.

"New semester. Don't wanna be late and paint a target on myself day one." Not even I was sold by my own excuse. I patted Kaju on the head. "You too, yeah? Watch for cars."

"You too, Oniisama." She beamed for a split second, then frowned. "Your tie is crooked." She righted the sin at once. Kaju and appearances. She peered up at me, tie still in her grip.

"What?"

"Perhaps it's my imagination, but I could have sworn I saw you grinning."

Grinning? About going to school? "I'm just so happy to see my little sister on this fine morning."

Kaju totally bought it and giggled. "We could always elope."

"I'm good. Got school." I opened the door and started on my way out. Kaju threw on a pair of sandals and gave chase. "What?"

"Stay right there. Don't turn around, please." I heard two hard clicks behind my shoulder. When I finally did turn around, Kaju was beaming again, a hunk of flint in one hand and a striker in the other. "For good luck. Have a good day, Oniisama."

***

I exited Aidai-Mae Station and joined the uniformed mob of fellow students. Conversations maintained a low drone over the crowd, though I wasn't the only one keeping to myself. So many different people. So many different faces. How many of them were genuine, I wondered.

Cutting the melodrama short, I slowed to part from the crowd and loosened the tie that Kaju had tried to strangle me with. A hand touched my back. "Good morning, Nukumizu-san."

Asagumo-san matched my pace. I choked on my words a couple times. "M-morning."

"I didn't know you took the train to school." If she knew I existed, she was already ahead of the curve. I failed to think of anything to reply with, so she held her chin up high and continued, "Better late than never, I suppose, but I had a real talk with Mitsuki-san and Lemon-san. I think it went well. I'm confident our relationships will be all the better for it."

"Oh. That's good," I said. And meant it, genuinely. I glanced around and leaned down to Asagumo-san's ear. "Hey, so, I've been meaning to ask..."

"Ask what?"

I lowered my voice. "Did you have one of those GPS trackers on Yakishio too?"

Asagumo-san made no apparent gesture that she'd even heard what I said. "I have a fun fact for you. Most small trackers have a limited battery life, typically lasting only a few days."

"Interesting." Was it?

"Now tell me. Would you still call a tracker a tracker, even without the ability to track? Or would junk be more accurate?" She tapped her finger against her chin a little too exaggeratedly and looked up at me. "What do you think?"

I would call such a device a dead tracker, but something told me this wasn't the hill to die on. I dropped it. "You're not at all the person I thought you'd be when we were in cram school together."

"Really? How so?"

"I dunno. I just thought you'd be all business. All refined and, well..."

I scoffed at myself. It sounded stupid saying it out loud. Making all those assumptions about someone I'd never even spoken to.

Asagumo-san grabbed my shoulder and stretched on her tiptoes to my ear. "We all have our dark sides, Nukumizu-san. Even me."

"Of that, I am aware."

Asagumo-san stifled a laugh. I started to crack a smirk when a hand touched my back a tad more violently than the first time.

"Morning, Chiha-chan! Morning, Nukkun!" cheered Yakishio. The look on her face betrayed none of the utter chaos and drama of the past week.

I smiled back awkwardly. "M-morning."

"Good morning, Lemon-san," greeted Asagumo-san.

Yakishio wedged herself between us. "Didn't think I'd find you two together. Sorry, Nukkun, but Chiha-chan's mine."

Chihaya. Chiha-chan. They'd sure gotten close fast.

"Hey, take her," I said.

"And thanks, by the way." Yakishio winked, then locked arms with her prey. "C'mon, let's go!"

"Of course," Asagumo-san acquiesced. "I'll see you later, Nukumizu-san."

They picked up the pace together.

"So hey, Chiha-chan, I can come borrow that shampoo you talked about today, right?"

"I won't be using the extra bottle anytime soon, so it's yours. I could even give you an entire routine, if you want."

If I didn't know better, I would have called that chemistry. Asagumo-san played with Yakishio's hair, and the latter didn't seem all too displeased about it. Scandalous. Immoral. More, please.

As I observed respectfully, I heard a bike creak to a stop behind me. A tall boy swung off it and came up next to me. "Morning, Nukumizu."

"Morning, Ayano."

Here came trouble. The source of it all. The neutron star himself—Ayano Mitsuki. Man, it was one after the other. Maybe that shop guy *had* turned me into a stamp rally checkpoint.

"So what's the deal with them?" I asked.

"Wish I could tell you. They've really hit it off." Ayano sighed. "You can bet Chihaya's heard every embarrassing story I have by now. What can you do, right?"

Ah, he was humblebragging again. It had only happened twice, but I was already sick of it. I made a mental note to be a little nicer to Yanami from now on.

"Cool. Give me time to escape the blast radius next time, please."

"Anyway." He threw his arm around my shoulder. "You tell me when you find the one. For real, this time. I'll be your wingman."

I couldn't think of a single person I'd want less as a wingman. How would I know when I found "the one," anyway? I considered my most available options...

Was it wrong of me to hope for better? The girls behind my phone screen didn't require half as much maintenance as they did.

Yakishio and Asagumo-san spotted Ayano and waved.

"Morning, Mitsuki!" the former called out.

"Good morning, Mitsuki-san," said Asagumo-san.

Mr. Popular waved back. "Morning, guys. Let's catch up to 'em, Nukumizu."

That sounded absolutely awful. I was already wiped, and I still had to put aside enough energy for whatever Yanami wanted after school.

"I'm gonna take my time," I said. "You go on without me."

"If you say so. See you later."

He and his merry band sauntered through the school gate. I took my sweet time doing the same. No one else was going to bother me. Once I got in that classroom, I would be zen.

"Boy..."

I stopped. Had someone just said something to me? I looked around but didn't see anyone I recognized. Must have been my imagination.

"Boy... Literature club boy."

Someone's breath tickled my ear, and my heart nearly leaped from my throat. Behind me, glued to my back like a shadow, was the student council's own Shikiya-san, who was looking sicklier than ever.

"Um, can I help you, Senpai?" She reached for my neck, her spindly fingers tightening around my tie. I froze. "H-hello?"

"First day... Already, your necktie is loose." Shikiya-san suddenly loosened her grip. She looked almost embarrassed. "Apologies. That was rude..." She pulled something off my collar and closed my hand around it. "Excuse me."

I was left with a single strand of black hair—Kaju's. How had it gotten there?

"Scatterbrained goober."

I let the hair go in the wind. While I watched Shikiya-san leave, it occurred to me that I'd never given back her handkerchief.

"N-Nukumizu... D-dare I ask what you're doing?"

"For the love of..." I was wasting my energy being surprised at this point. "Forget it. Hey, Komari." She had ridden up on a bike. The white helmet looked good on her. An objective improvement, in my humble opinion. "Shikiya-senpai was fiddling with my uniform."

"B-before that. With the g-guy."

"That was Ayano from Class D. He's been to the club room before."

Komari wasn't listening. "First the delinquent," she muttered. "Then...the honor student." She got that twinkle in her eye. There she went again.

"Hakamada's not a delinquent, first of all. Second of all, keep your fantasies to yourself, pretty please."

"Is it a s-secret?" Komari was off to the races. She started blushing and grinning, which I hated because it was kinda cute.

"It is neither secret nor public because there is nothing to *be* secret or public. I'm leaving before you make me late."

I left her for the shoe cupboards.

Day one of the new semester was already off to an exhausting start. I was going to have to start coming to school earlier.

***

After school. The fire escape at the old annex. I was staring out over the campus grounds with Yanami, the pleasant September breeze carrying away the last of the summer heat.

"So you didn't think to update me because...?" Yanami tore open the packaging on an Ogura sandwich from a local bakery. She was not happy.

I stabbed a straw into my milk. "You never asked. And in my defense, it wasn't my info to share."

"It never occurred to you that maybe I had a horse in this race? Like, they kinda *made* it my business." She took an aggressive bite then plopped her elbows on the railing. "Whatever. All's well that ends well, I suppose. So long as Lemon-chan's happy."

The track team was warming up out across the field. We could make out the echoes of an admonishment being hurled at a certain tan girl for trying to skip stretching.

"She's definitely better," I said. "At the very least, she can handle the rest by herself." Yakishio had settled things on her own, in her own way. We'd had no part in that. In all matters of love, no matter its form, it really did come down to the parties involved. "Anyway, what happened to no more snacking?"

Gulping down the last of her sandwich, Yanami clapped her hands together. "I've won, Nukumizu-kun."

"Congrats." I had a bad feeling about this already.

Yanami didn't care. "I lost 250 grams in a week, proving the efficacy of my strategy."

That...really wasn't a lot. "Did you try another scale?"

"Don't you see? That's a whole kilogram per month. The universe has granted me victory, Nukumizu-kun." And me defeat for saying something in the first place. I *uh-huh*'d her, utterly detached. "But here's the problem. On a larger scale, that means losing *twelve kilograms* in a year, which may be potentially problematic health-wise."

She had problems, all right. With her brain.

"So here's the deal," Yanami went on, pseudo-intellectualist conceit oozing off her every word. "I keep doing what I'm doing, but if I cancel it out by eating enough to *gain* a kilogram per month, I'll maintain my weight perfectly. Am I a genius or what?"

"Yanami-san, I'm begging you to think about what you just said. Does any of that actually make sense?" Unfortunately, even I was too human to abandon her to her fate.

Even more unfortunately, Yanami nodded without a shred of doubt. "The scale doesn't lie, Nukumizu-kun. And yes, I did the math. One kilogram of fat is roughly equal to 7,200 calories. That's at least twenty cups of ramen. I've got a lot of catching up to do." She cracked open a package of bread. "Sho bayshkly mhtegly shilldyding." She swallowed (a few seconds too late, if you asked me). "I'm a visionary, dude. I've got the numbers to back me up. Man, I should write a book."

"Save one for me so I can have your autograph."

She would learn. One day. The numbers wouldn't lie.

I sipped some milk, spacing out. Classes were off to an exceptionally normal start. They'd done a good job at shaking the last of that vacation fog. Back to routine.

Unrelatedly, Amanatsu-sensei's Obon gamble hadn't played out—she was still single, and she made sure we all knew that.

"Forgot Prez said the journal was done. Should go grab that," I said.

"Oh, I did that already." Yanami dug in her bag. "Here. Snagged one for you."

Two men gazed longingly at each other on the cover. The clothing in particular seemed like a rush job. One could only wonder what the artist's original intent had been.

I flipped through it. "Wow, I can't believe Tsukinoki-senpai actually got hers in." I skipped through the pages until something made me pause.

An entry for Yakishio's picture diary.

The caption described us coming to visit her at her grandma's. The illustration depicted the five of us all packed into a car, headed toward what looked to be a fairy-tale style castle. Presumably, the markings on the castle walls were meant to be the Tsuwabuki school emblem. I chose to let slide the fact that Yakishio had never actually been in the car with us.

I turned the page. Yanami's story was next. Her previous work had been a bittersweet tale of love and karaage skewers. This next one had me curious. Ignoring all propriety, being literally right next to her and all, I read.

Literature Club Summer Activity Report: Yanami

Anna—A Good Morning

Here I am, reading my magazines at the convenience store again. Well, pretending to, really. This corner of the 7-Eleven is where I have the best view of the intersection he always crosses every morning.

I'm going to tell him good morning. I know I will. And who knows? Maybe we'll even walk to school together!

An intoxicating scent wafts by me just then. The clerk announces to the store, "Smoked arabiki sausage! Get it while it's hot!"

7-Eleven is my weakness. Their snacks are just that good.

Their arabiki sausage is all natural. You can tell by the texture and the way the casing pops when you bite into it. And don't get me started on that smoky aroma. It stirs up an appetite like nothing else. And they're not too heavy for a morning snack either.

Usually they're done earlier. They're never fresh this late in the day.

I still don't see him, so I make a run for it. Of all the days for there to be a line at the register. It feels like forever before it's finally my turn.

"One smoked arabiki sausage, please!"

"That'll be 116 yen."

"I should have exact change."

I open my wallet to check, and the automatic doors slide open. I hear his laugh. He's waiting at the intersection with his friends.

The light turns green.

"No bag, please!"

I take my sausage on a stick and try to put away my wallet, but I can't. My hands are full. Every second I waste, he gets further away.

I stuff the sausage into my mouth and run out the doors just as they start to close. (Author's Note: Do not run with food in your mouth.)

I have to say it.

"***-kun, good mo—!"

The sausage falls from my mouth, but I catch it in midair. The light turns red, and my shoulders fall. He's long gone, laughing with his friends.

Another morning without a "good morning."

My sausage didn't taste quite as good after that.

***

I was suddenly accosted by an inexplicable craving for sausages.

"I like your story," I said. "Your passion for sausage really shines through."

"Really? Man, I'm glad I went and tried some myself for research, then." Yanami finished off her bread, then got real serious. "Hey. Nukumizu-kun."

"Yeah? What's up?"

"I have a boyfriend now."

Wow. Okay. That was sudden. "Congrats?"

"Except I don't." Well, which was it? Yanami groaned. "I think I fished a little too hard on Instagram. All my friends think I'm seeing someone now, and they want to meet him..."

"Tell them you do not have a boyfriend."

"I can't!" she snapped. "I'm in too deep. I made my little breadcrumb trail of bait, and now I need to follow through or everyone'll think I got dumped again!"

"Dumped? Again?"

Far as I recalled, she'd never made it that far.

She looked at me, a sneaky glint in her eye. "So I had an idea. Why not get myself a *cover boy*?"

"A cover boy."

"A cover boy. Just someone to show off and be all, 'Heh,' y'know?"

So a fake boyfriend. Now, which rom-com had I seen that trope in?

I definitely wasn't interested, but I was a *little* interested, if that made sense. "Clever."

"I know, right? So anyway, I had a favor to ask you."

Call me crazy, but I had a feeling I knew where this was going. As extremely disinterested as I was in playing boyfriend, an innocent part of me did find the prospect of living out one of my light novels appealing.

"What kind of favor?" I asked, head tilted at a perfect forty-five degree angle. Nailed it.

Yanami leaned in. "I know this is asking a lot."

"U-uh-huh?"

She leaned in closer. "Can you ask Ayano-kun if he'd be interested?! He's hot *and* smart! He'd literally be perfect."

"Are you for real right now?"

She looked pretty for real.

I rested my elbows on the railing and let the first whispers of fall caress my cheek. What a summer it had been. I prayed this new semester wouldn't be half as eventful.

"So?" Yanami leaned against the rail with me. "Think you can do that for me?"

I knew what I thought. I gave her my most polite smile and told her.

"How about you find your own boyfriend?"

When Your Sister Might Have Problems

I STOOD AT THE FRONT DOOR, BACK HOME AFTER MY impromptu trip to Shinshiro. I'd gotten permission from my parents to spend the night, so that wasn't what worried me. No, what gave me pause was something else entirely.

Kaju.

She never liked me being away for long. She got lonely. Our mom had to physically hold her back to keep her from chasing after me at the train station during a field trip back in junior high. To make matters worse, I hadn't heard a single peep from her in almost twenty-four hours.

I took a deep breath and opened the door. "I'm home," I called out hesitantly, then bent over to take off my shoes.

In came running an apron-clad Kaju. "Oniisama! Welcome back!"

"H-hey, Kaju."

She was in a good mood. Odd.

"What're you standing around for? Come in! Would you like lunch first? A bath? Or maybe... Oh, Oniisama, we *mustn't*!" Kaju grabbed my face and squished and pinched my cheeks.

What was happening right now?

"You didn't eat any wild mushrooms out of the garden, did you?"

"You are such a jokester, Oniisama. Do you have any laundry? I'll take care of all that for you."

"I'll, uh, bring it over later. I'm gonna go change first."

"Of course! I'll get on lunch!" Off she scurried.

Again. What? A question I would have to answer after getting settled, first and foremost.

I made it up to my room and was pulling my shirt off when I noticed a bunch of stuff crammed onto my desk.

"Books?"

Probably the ones I'd lended her. I reached for one and froze solid almost immediately. They were books all right. Ones I had kept purposefully hidden on account of their titles.

Who Says Little Sisters Can't Have Their Own Rom-Coms?

That Time I Told My Sister Siblings Can Get Married for a Laugh and She Took Me Seriously.

I Can Act Spoiled If My Little Sister Is Older than Me, Right?

I Think My Sister and I Aren't Blood-Related, but That's None of My Business.

My Sister Has Problems.

These were titles Kaju was never meant to see. All sister-related light novels went as far back behind my dresser as they could go.

I could explain, of course. Sometimes a particular book would be accredited for, say, the Upcoming Light Novel Award, and sometimes I would buy them out of curiosity, and sometimes they would *happen* to be about sisters. That was all there was to it. Seriously. On my life, it was not a *thing*.

The question remained, though.

"What are they doing out here?" My camouflage had been perfect.

Hands trembling, I picked one up. It was worse than I thought. Several pages were bookmarked with sticky notes.

But marking what?

As I began to open the book, morbid curiosity getting the better of me, I sensed a pair of eyes boring into me.

I whipped around. "Kaju!"

She stood on the other side of a door that had been closed just seconds prior. Smiling. "Lunch is ready, Oniisama."

"O-okay. Be right there." I replaced the book on my desk and followed her to the living room. I would cross this bridge after food.

And figure out a better hiding spot.

Too Many Losing Heroines!

Afterword

LONG TIME NO READ. IT'S TAKIBI AMAMORI.

Wow, two volumes of losing heroines. You'd think they couldn't lose anymore, but here we are, thanks to all of your support. This time around, we're giving the spotlight to the only one who didn't get a chance to really shine—our lovely Lemon-chan.

It truly is an honor to be given the opportunity to depict life after-the-fact for heroines both lucky and unlucky.

Imigimuru-sensei really hit it out of the park with Asagumo-san, considering she only had a short cameo in Volume 1. Shikiya-san as well. Who knows what's going on inside that head of hers. Actually, maybe she was there all along? Scary thought.

I certainly tried Mr. Iwaasa's patience with this volume. His guidance had us bouncing drafts back and forth all the way up to the deadline, which was surely a nightmare for Imigimuru-sensei when things inevitably came in late. My apologies to everyone affected by the crunch, and my thanks for nonetheless producing such a quality final product.

The existence of which I owe to you, the readers. Largely for buying my book, yes, but also in part because a story is only truly a story when experienced. That's right. You, the reader, are responsible for breathing life into Team Failgirl via the stage in your head.

Loyalty to the cause is voluntary, of course, but I hope you'll stick with us.

If another volume is in the cards, we'll join a slightly more mature Nukumizu-kun for his second semester. Rest assured, there will be plenty of losers. I hope they'll have your company as they figure out this thing called life.

Now, I was given a rather generous number of pages to write this afterword. I considered filling them with talk about my health and my age and that one time I counted it wrong, thereby consecrating me a year younger (if only that was how it worked). Even got about halfway through that idea, but I stopped because I, an adult, have that power.

So if you flip back a few pages, you can see I made the grown-up decision to dedicate them to the interlude I never got to fit into the main story. It takes place directly after Loss 3 and doesn't *really* have any bearing on the plot, but hey. Consider it behind the scenes.

ABOUT THE AUTHOR

Takibi Amamori

Thrilled to be able to bring you a continuation in the lives of the Losing Heroines, and glad to have you share it with them.